THE BEASTS OF
STONECLAD
MOUNTAIN

GERRY GRIFFITHS

SEVERED PRESS
HOBART TASMANIA

THE BEASTS OF STONECLAD MOUNTAIN

ISBN: 978-1-925597-64-6

DEDICATION
For my daughter, Genene

1

James Payne lounged in his lawn chair under the overhang of the cave, reading one of his Louis L'Amour westerns. The paperback was missing the front cover, and the pages were about to fall out of the spine, but that didn't deter him from continuing the saga of the marshal single-handedly trying to protect the townsfolk from the ruthless outlaw gang.

He flipped the page, bumping his elbow against the barrel of his 30-shot magazine Bushmaster automatic rifle leaning against the armrest.

It could hardly be called a sporting hunting gun—more of an essential weapon for protecting one's property.

He took a break from his book, dog-eared the page, and tossed the reading material onto the backpack just inside the cave. The cavern went back twenty feet, was ten feet wide, and was high enough to walk upright to the rear of the hollowed rock.

Marijuana stalks hung from clotheslines stretched across the width of the cave, the ends anchored to carabiners wedged in the crevices in the walls. A large blue tarpaulin was on the ground where James would bring in his lawn chair and trim the buds off the stalks. A couple canvas picking sacks with neck straps were on the ground next to some tilling spades, shovels, rakes, and hoes leaning against the cavern wall.

He had a modest setup for cooking: a frying pan and a pot for boiling water and a double-burner portable Coleman camp stove. For lighting at night, he had one flashlight and a kerosene lantern. His sleeping accommodations consisted of a dirty mummy goose-down bag on top of an inflatable air mattress that demanded to be frequently filled up with air with a foot pump as it had a slow leak.

Besides preparing the next shipment for transport down the mountain, eating, sleeping, and suffering mind-numbing cabin fever, even though he was in the great outdoors and it was a cave, there wasn't much more for James to do during his solitary five-day durations sharing the duties of the family business, other than to read.

James raised his arms and stretched. He got up from his chair, leaving the slumped webbing in the shape of his butt.

He glanced out at the lush field of ten-foot-tall marijuana plants—last count there were somewhere over two hundred—clustered tightly together, surrounded by the dense forest of broad-leaf bur oaks and white pines.

It was the perfect spot for cultivating weed. The soil was rich, and it was secluded, an arduous four-hour hike up the steep and treacherous mountain, miles away from the nearest farm. James thought it was overkill having to climb so far up the mountain, but that was how his eldest brother, Landon, wanted it, so what choice did he have?

And there was no worry of hikers or campers stumbling onto their operation, as there were no proper trails in the rough terrain. Nothing on the mountain, but abandoned moonshine stills, more natural caves and forgotten mineshafts, and maybe the occasional reclusive hermit that didn't want to be bothered by civilization and could care less about the Payne brothers' moneymaking venture.

While James spent most of his lonely hours on the mountain, reading, his other three brothers could care less about books, especially the twins, Jacob and Mason, who would rather drink moonshine and play mumblety-peg barefoot—even though Mason had self-amputated two of his own toes with bad knife throws from being too drunk to care, and his lack of depth perception because of his one eye.

But James knew better than to talk down to Jacob and Mason as each of his brothers weighed over two hundred fifty pounds and looked like true mountain men with their rough appearances and wooly beards. Their jobs were, when the time arose, hauling the packs of hemp down the mountain.

James' older brother, Landon, was head of the family business and was in charge of distribution. Only on rare occasions did he come up to the field.

James was glad that this would be his last night on the mountain until his next time around. All he could think of when he was up here alone, were his brothers carousing at home, getting drunk on two hundred proof pure grain alcohol and having a good time.

Sometimes they got out of hand, but Landon quickly interceded, as he swore he'd be damned if he'd let them drink themselves blind.

Though it was another hour before sunset, daylight seemed to wane under the dense forest canopy. He figured he better prepare for nightfall and light the lantern inside the cave. For dinner, he planned on eating some pulled pork and heating a pot of corn kernels on the camp stove.

That's when he heard something moving about out in the field.

The tall plants swayed, as whatever it was, cut a path behind the rows.

James reached down and picked up his Bushmaster. He tucked the butt stock into his shoulder and aimed the weapon, aligning the front sight on any intended target that might show itself.

By the heavy, scuffling footfalls, it sounded big. There were a few black bears in the area, but they always seemed to keep their distance. Normally, he would be alarmed, but he felt confident holding his assault rifle. Besides, he knew not to back down from a bear and that they could be easily intimidated if he acted aggressive.

"Come on, Mr. Bear. Show yourself," he taunted.

The plants continued to move.

He clicked off the safety, slipped his forefinger inside the trigger guard.

"I'm warning you!"

He heard a rustle and then everything went still.

James approached the field, slowly, one cautious step followed by another, ready to fire at the smallest provocation. He squeezed down a row. The ripe-for-harvest milky-white buds on the plants gave off a skunk-like odor.

He used the muzzle of his assault rifle to prod back the leaves and then stopped to listen.

A distracting breeze picked up, rustling the leaves in the surrounding trees.

"This is your last chance! You better get!"

A dark figure lurched out from behind the plants on his left. James swung the barrel of his gun around and pulled back the trigger as the thing dove back into the marijuana bushes for cover.

The bullets strafed the tops off the plants.

James heard a loud grunt followed by an ear-piercing primordial scream that was so loud it echoed through the forest. He tried to rationalize what he had just seen. It had all happened so fast. It had been enormous, covered with thick, grayish fur.

That was no bear. A bear would have kept charging, plunged him into the ground, and mauled the life out of him with its sharp claws. This creature seemed to sense danger the moment he pointed his gun.

Whatever it was, James knew he had hit it, as there was blood splatter on the leaves of one of the plants.

And then he heard a tormented yowl.

Ice water jetted through his veins. Even though he was brandishing a high-caliber weapon, James felt somewhat unprotected, like somehow the situation had reversed, and he had suddenly become the prey.

An arm swung out from behind the tall foliage and cuffed him upside the temple with such a tremendous blow that it almost took off his head. He fell back and landed on the hard ground, dropping his rifle during the fall.

Flat on his back, James gazed up, struggling to catch a breath as the impact had knocked the air out of his lungs. Blood seeped into his eyes, blurring his vision.

The leathery sole of a giant foot hovered over James' face then stomped down.

James screamed as his forearm snapped on his right arm. It was like someone had dropped an anvil on him from a considerable height. He glanced over and saw the contrasting white of a spear tip of bone sticking out of his brown coat sleeve.

A black-furred beast came down on top of him, smothering him with its thick, pungent coat. James gagged and reached up, grabbing a handful of coarse, matted hair.

With his face buried in the noxious hair, and still not knowing what was attacking him, James felt his left ankle seized by a powerful hand and his leg lifted off the ground.His leg began to twist in a circular motion, and kept on turning, forcing tendons and muscle to tear as his kneecap ground out of the socket and the toe of his boot pointed in a ridiculous direction.

James had never felt such pain, not even while his abusive, psychopath father beat him within an inch of his life when he was ten years old.

"Please…oh God…please stop…" he cried.

And then, if it was even possible, the pain further increased when his leg was wrenched out of his pelvis, and a wet gush poured over his groin.

His attacker grunted, and then James heard something cast into the air and land somewhere off in the field.

Even buried under the tremendous weight of his thickly furred assailant, James' body went cold as he rapidly bled out, the bright red seepage draining into the rich, furrowed soil.

He thought of his brothers, wishing he were home, reading a western, as he gazed up for the last time into the humongous gaping mouth, filled with broad tombstone teeth, bearing down on his face.

2

"I think Casey needs changing," Mia said, scrunching up her nose.

"We're almost there," Clay replied. He kept one hand on the wheel and cranked his window down a bit to let in some fresh air. He shot a glance in the rearview mirror and saw Casey strapped in his car seat surrounded by a laundry basket of clothes and some suitcases. His one-year-old son looked pleased with himself, content to stare out the window and watch the world go by.

Hell, that boy could lay some stinkers.

"How's he doing on diapers?" Clay asked, knowing that even if there was a store somewhere out on this endless road out in the middle of nowhere, which he doubted, he didn't have much cash. Most of it had gone into the tank of the Cutlass just getting out here.

"You know where you're going?" Mia asked.

He knew she wasn't nagging him. She wasn't the sort. It was just that there hadn't been any road signs to follow and the countryside was looking pretty much the same after a while. "Sure. I was out here plenty of times when I was a kid."

"How old were you then?"

"I don't know, maybe six. It all still looks the same."

Mia stared out her window. "So you haven't seen your uncle in fifteen years?"

"That'd be about right."

"Sure glad your mom wrote him that letter."

Clay stayed to the right when he came to a fork in the road. "I wish she hadn't, but what can we do? Hard to get a good job if you don't have a trade."

"What does your uncle do?"

"Handyman mostly."

Clay gunned the Oldsmobile up a dirt road and stopped at the top of a grassy hillock. To the east was the mountain range of forest with hundreds of miles of rough, impenetrable terrain that seemed to stretch right up to the clouds.

A small, shingled-roofed cabin with a railing porch and stone chimney was down below, butted up to the edge of the woods.

Not too far away was a neglected twenty-foot singlewide trailer in a patch of foot-high weeds.

A silver antenna was mounted on the top of a mast, ten feet above the roof. The siding was rusted and it had a large dent near the front. One of the windows had a cracked windowpane. Three wood steps were below the door. The base of the mobile home was mostly trimmed with lattice to hide the underneath, but Clay could see some of the cinderblocks supporting the structure off the ground.

"So, that's it?" Mia said, assessing the trailer.

"Could use some fixing up," Clay had to admit. It would take some work. A lot of work, but who were they to look a gift horse in the mouth. From what he understood, Uncle Ethan was just helping them out as a favor to Clay's mom. Times were hard, everyone knew that, but you never turned your back on family.

"We should stop by the cabin and let Uncle Ethan know we're here. Then we can go to the trailer and change the little poop monster." Clay looked over his shoulder at Casey. "Bet you'd like that."

His son grinned as he squirmed his tiny butt in the car seat.

Clay didn't envy Mia's job one bit.

He drove down and parked in front of the cabin. Mia got out first and unbuckled Casey, taking him out of his car seat. "Whew. I'm sorry, Clay, but I've got to clean him up before we meet your uncle."

"All right, then." Clay got out and looked around. The scenery was beautiful, that is if he ignored that monstrosity of a trailer.

Mia laid Casey on the front seat and undid the pins on his cloth diaper. She held onto Casey's ankles and lifted him up. She removed the soiled diaper and dropped it on the ground, then grabbed some wipes out of the diaper bag and cleaned the boy up.

Clay walked up the front steps onto the porch and sauntered over to the front door. A slip of paper was hanging on a nail.

"Uncle Ethan left us a note," Clay said in a loud voice so Mia could hear. "Says he'll be back soon, that we should go on in and make ourselves at home. Feel free to eat something if we're hungry." He looked over and saw Mia pick up the dirty diaper off the ground and slip it inside a plastic bag. "Better seal that up good," he said, giving his wife a smile though he could tell she wasn't too thrilled when she shot him a scowl.

"Are you hungry, sweetie?" Mia asked Casey as she lifted him off the seat and toted him in her arms.

Casey cooed and reached his mischievous hand into Mia's shirt.

"Just hold your horses, mister."

Clay turned the doorknob and pushed the door open. He waited for Mia and Casey before stepping inside. The front room was somewhat dark, as there was only one window, so Clay left the door open. A chair and settee with matching cushions faced the stone hearth. A large trunk covered with a small blanket served as a coffee table.

Two rifles hung on hooks above the mantle over the fireplace. A large reddish throw rug covered a good portion of the planked floor.

In a corner was a cedar hutch with glass cabinet doors on the top and drawers with more doors on the bottom section.

To the side was the kitchen area. A sink, with a hand pump for drawing water, stood under the window. The wall was lined with shelves. Pots and fry pans were in easy reach on the bottom, food sacks and boxes, and canned goods taking up the other shelves.

There was a black, cast-iron, wood-burning cook stove with a smokestack going up through the timbered ceiling, and a small dining table with two matching chairs made out of a dark wood, and a white pine chair.

"I don't see a fridge," Mia commented.

"That's because there's no electricity," Clay replied. "There's no power company out here."

Casey started crying. "All right," Mia said, in an impatient tone. She carried the infant across the room and sat in the chair by the fireplace. She unbuttoned her shirt and drew out a breast for Casey to suckle even though she was finding it increasingly difficult to produce enough breast milk to satisfy her hungry baby's insatiable appetite.

Mia looked up at Clay. "We're almost out of formula."

"Maybe there's some evaporated milk." Clay went over to the kitchen. He heard a vehicle approaching outside and looked out the window. A blue International Scout truck pulled up and stopped just outside the cabin. "It's Uncle Ethan." He turned and looked over at Mia. "You better button up."

Mia pushed Casey off and fumbled with her shirt. Casey grabbed hold of a button and refused to let go.

"Casey, stop," she snapped.

Clay watched his uncle step out of his truck, followed by a large dog with a black head and droopy ears and a body covered with black ticking and large spots. The dog paraded alongside the tall man up the porch steps.

Mia was still struggling to close up her shirt, trying to discourage Casey's persistent fingers.

"Hurry," Clay whispered as the cabin door opened.

"Well, hi there…" Ethan said as he came in then stopped short when he saw Mia frantically trying to cover up. He politely turned away and looked over at Clay.

"Glad you made it," he said.

"I'm so sorry," Mia apologized, having to smack Casey's hand so she could make herself presentable.

"That's quite all right," Ethan replied.

Clay came over and shook his uncle's hand. "Thank you for giving us a place to stay." He always looked up to his uncle, one reason being that the barrel-chested man stood six-foot-five and reminded him of the actor Clint Walker that played in that old TV western, *Cheyenne*.

"My pleasure. How is Erma…I mean, your mom?"

"She's doing fine."

"Good to hear."

Clay looked at the doorway and saw the dog sitting obediently just outside the threshold on the porch. "That's a good-looking dog. What's his name?"

"That there's Blu. Got him from Alberta Blake. She's a breeder of blue tick coonhounds and sort of the vet around these parts."

"Is he a good hunting dog?" Clay asked.

"Well, he's learning. Most time he's too distracted."

"Don't they just naturally pick it up?" Mia asked.

"Not Blu. When he was born, he came out bottom first and isn't quite right."

"What's wrong with him?" Clay asked.

"He has seizures."

"Is he all right now?"

"I hope so. He hasn't had one for a few months."

"How do you think he'd be around Casey?" Mia asked.

"Your little boy? How about we see?" Ethan turned and slapped his hand against his thigh. "Blu. Come!"

The coonhound immediately got to his feet, pranced into the cabin and went directly over to Mia and Casey, and sat down beside the chair. He rested his chin on the armrest and looked up at Mia with an expectant gaze.

"Give him a head rub," Ethan told Mia.

Mia held Casey tight and reached over with her other hand.

"But I'd be careful."

Mia quickly withdrew her hand. "Why? He won't bite?"

"No, but your hand might fall off giving him those rubs."

Mia smiled and scratched the top of Blu's head.

"So what do you think?" Ethan said.

"Thanks for the use of the trailer," Clay replied.

"Trailer? I'm talking about the cabin."

"You're letting us stay here?" Mia said.

"Uncle Ethan, we can't do that." Generosity was one thing, but Clay couldn't expect his uncle to give up his place.

"Son, I insist. Besides, this place is too big for one person."

Clay looked around and saw only one other door, which he figured led into a bedroom.

"But this is your home," Clay said.

"Now it's yours, as long as you want. Besides, it gives me a chance to fix up that old trailer. Been wanting to do it for some time, but never had a reason to. Now I do."

Mia stood. "We don't know how to thank you."

"Don't mention it. I have to go. Got a fence to mend." Ethan slapped his thigh and Blu came running. He waved over his shoulder as he went down the stairs. He went over to the truck, opened the door for Blu to jump in, and climbed behind the wheel.

Clay watched as he drove off.

"I feel so bad," Mia said.

"Uncle Ethan has a big heart." Clay walked over, opened the bedroom door, and looked into the room. "Mia, come see this."

Next to the bed was a handcrafted pinewood crib.

3

It wasn't until Caleb Dribble completed coming around the bend that he saw the fallen tree in the headlights, blocking the road. He stomped on the brake, shoving the pedal clear down to the floorboard. The rear tires locked up as the old Chevy truck shook like it was going to come apart, skidding across the hard-packed dirt.

The front steel bumper collided into the tree. Caleb flung against the steering wheel. A loud squeal sounded from the bed of the truck, followed by a heavy crash against the outside of the cab. Caleb winced from his bruised ribs, turned, and gazed over his shoulder through the rear window that was protected by a metal mesh screen.

The butcher hog was thrashing about inside the livestock cage, frightened by the jarring impact. In this state, and weighing over three hundred pounds, the swine was extremely dangerous as it slammed against one side of the steel enclosure then rammed against the opposite side, rocking the truck like a canoe about to capsize.

"Simmer down!" Caleb yelled, furious that the swine was going to injure itself and ruin the meat before he could make the exchange. A pig this size was worth a couple months' worth of feed and cornmeal. It would hardly seem a fair trade if he were to deliver a dead animal that was beaten to a pulp.

"I said, quiet down!" But it was useless to try and reason with the frightened animal.

It was then that Caleb realized the engine had quit. The right headlight was out as a tree limb had bashed out the lamp. He turned the ignition key to restart the truck. The single headlight dimmed as the starter motor whined, but the engine refused to turn over. He switched off the headlight and tried again. This time, he heard a clicking sound under the hood and knew he had drained the battery.

"Oh, come on!" he yelled, slamming the top of the steering wheel with the palm of his hand.

The hog continued to batter itself inside the cage.

Caleb reached for the handle and rolled down the window.

"Shut the hell up!"

It was nearing sunrise so there was just enough twilight illuminating the woods around him so that he could just make out the faint silhouettes of the red alders and birch trees on both sides of the road.

He reached under the bench seat and felt around in the dark. His hand swiped a few empty pint bottles that clinked against one another until he found the heavy cudgel that he sometimes used to conk uncontrollable pigs and knock them unconscious but not enough to kill them. He knew it would be suicide to step inside the livestock cage with the animal as it could pin him up against the steel bars, and if it didn't crush him to death, it would surely not waste any time making a meal out of him.

Hogs were known man-eaters.

Caleb figured he could stand beside the truck, and once the porker was close enough, he could reach in and club the animal on the head. Shut the damn thing up.

As he grabbed for the door handle, he glanced at the side mirror mounted on the outside of the door.

A huge figure stood by the rear fender. It had to be eight feet tall as its head was the same height as the top of the livestock enclosure. Caleb reached for the knob to wind up the window then froze when he saw the thing moving toward the driver's side of the truck.

Caleb edged away from the window and scooted slowly across the seat. Even with all the hog's hurly-burly, he could still hear the approach of heavy footfalls. As it got closer, Caleb could smell the creature, a musky stench, as vile as an outhouse's crapper pit.

A huge, black fur-covered hand clamped its fat fingers down on the window frame of the door. It was three times the size of

Caleb's hand and looked like a gorilla's with chipped brown fingernails instead of claws.

Caleb was trying everything imaginable not to scream, especially when the door buckled as it was pulled out, snapping off the locking mechanism. The door remained on its hinges and swung out a few inches then stopped as the hand let go and disappeared into the darkness.

Caleb retreated to the other side of the cab and raised his heavy stick in a feeble defense. He glanced into the side mirror on the passenger door.

Another creature was standing by the rear bumper on that side of the truck.

"Oh, Jesus."

The hog was going crazy, sensing a new danger.

Caleb stared in the side mirror and watched in horror as the monstrous beast grabbed the steel door to the cage and tore it off the hinges. When the creature's image in the side mirror disappeared behind the truck, Caleb turned and looked out through the rear window of the cab.

Caleb watched as the hog was dragged out of the cage. He looked back at the side mirror. One of the creatures was holding the flailing hog up by one of its hind legs—all three hundred pounds—dangling it with only one hand.

The hog squealed as it struggled to get free.

Then, with one mighty swing, the creature slammed the hog up against the side of the pickup, killing it instantly.

Caleb heard the limp body fall to the ground. There were fierce snarls and the rendering of flesh as slopping innards plashed on the dirt.

The carnage continued on for more than ten minutes. Caleb was too frightened to move. After they were through ripping apart the hog, he feared he would be next.

He closed his eyes, trembling, waiting for the inevitable.

But after a few more minutes, he couldn't hear anything but songbirds chirping as dawn broke through the trees.

Caleb pushed open the door and stepped from the truck. He walked warily around to the back. A blood trail of gore led into the woods.

He started to run, slowly at first, then faster and kept on running, the entire two miles back to the hog farm, never once stopping.

4

A man's voice called out, "Ethan, come in. This is Roth, over."

Ethan tried to roll over in his bed but something was pressed up against his chest, preventing him from moving.

Again, the man's voice boomed in the small trailer. "Ethan, pick up!"

Ethan opened his eyes and saw that it wasn't even daylight yet. He sat up in the queen-size bed that took up almost the entire bedroom. He glanced down and saw Blu sprawled out, still fast asleep.

"If I have to get up, so do you," he said, and gave Blu a slap on the rump.

Instead of awakening with alarm, the coonhound opened his eyes gradually and stretched out his legs.

"Lazy bones." Ethan crawled across to the foot of the bed and stepped into the hallway. He passed the bathroom and closet and went into the living area where a battery-operated shortwave radio was sitting on a small table in front of the couch. Ethan picked up the hand mike and pressed the talk button.

"What is it, Roth? Over."

The speaker crackled and then Roth said, "I need you to come out and clear my road. Can you do that? Over."

"Sure. When?" Ethan asked, clicking off his microphone.

"As soon as you can."

"I'll be out there in an hour."

"An hour's good. Over and out."

Ethan tossed the mike on the table. "Blu! Get your sorry self up!"

He turned on the propane stove and placed a coffee pot on the burner. Walking back to the closet, he grabbed a shirt, a pair of jeans, and boots, got dressed, and went into the living area.

Ethan was pouring himself a cup of coffee when Blu finally joined him, yawning and stopping to scratch his side with his rear paw.

"About time."

He filled a thermos with coffee, and put some peppered pemmican into a paper sack for later. He drank some more coffee and put the cup down on the drain board.

After he slipped a black woolen cap on his head, he put on a heavy jacket. He grabbed his Colt Sauer thirty-ought-six and tucked the rifle under his arm. As soon as he opened the door of the trailer, the frigid air funneling down off the mountain hit him in the face like a wintry slap. He turned up his collar and let Blu pass before he closed the door and went down the steps.

Ethan went over to the truck, opened the driver's door. Blu jumped in and curled up on the freezing vinyl in the middle of the bench seat. Ethan put his rifle on the gun rack mounted over the rear window.

He got in and started the engine, switching on the defroster as the cold engine idled. Satisfied that the engine had warmed up, he put the transmission into gear and drove over to the cabin.

He got out leaving the door open, went up to the cabin's front door, and gave it a couple heavy thumps. "Clay! Get up, son!" He waited for a few seconds more then pounded again. "Time for work!"

He could hear footsteps in the cabin.

The door slowly opened and Clay peered out. "Uncle Ethan?"

"Grab some clothes. We've got a job."

"Uh, yes, sir. Be right out."

Ethan let out a sharp whistle. "Blu, get over here."

The dog jumped down from the cab and ran around the front of the truck and dashed up on the porch.

"You stay here."

Blu lay on the porch by the front door, with his head down on his front paws.

"That's a boy."

Ethan walked back to the truck and got behind the wheel. He liked that his nephew hadn't balked. He almost had to laugh when Clay came bumbling out, almost stumbling over Blu, as he tried fastening up his trousers with one arm in his jacket. He hopped on one foot not having his boot on right and opened the passenger door. He climbed in and shut the door.

"Morning, Uncle Ethan."

"Didn't interrupt anything, did I?"

Clay gave him a shocked look as he shivered.

"Just funning with you, son."

Clay glanced out the passenger window. "You leaving Blu here?"

"Thought you might like him watching over your family."

"Thanks, Uncle Ethan."

"Here, this should warm you up." Ethan handed Clay the thermos.

Clay removed the cap, unscrewed the stopper, and poured a cup of steaming coffee. He took a sip and held the cup with both hands to get some warmth.

"Mind you don't spill," Ethan said, stepping on the accelerator as they headed up the hill.

"Mia and I really appreciate you letting us stay in your place. Casey slept like a rock in that crib you made."

"Glad to hear that," Ethan said, taking a turn and heading up a rutted road that snaked through the trees. The stiff suspension and the oversized all-terrain snow tires on the International Scout made for a bumpy ride, especially whenever Ethan had to change gears when the cambered track got tricky whenever the throughway narrowed. The last thing he wanted was to bottom out on the drive shaft and screw up the u-joints.

"What's up in here?" Clay asked, finishing his coffee and putting the cap back on the thermos.

"Roth Becker's hog farm. Called me on the shortwave this morning. Needs us to help clear his road."

Ethan slammed on the brakes as they made a turn. The truck rattled as the big tires locked up and the Scout stopped short of hitting the tree lying across the road.

The livestock truck was parked on the other side with its hood up. Roth and Caleb were both in front of the grill, bent over the engine compartment.

"Come on, I'll introduce you," Ethan said, opening his door. Clay got out on his side. They walked over to the fallen tree. The trunk was three feet in diameter, the limbs and branches tapering up, the topmost part toppled into the brush.

Ethan and clay climbed over and walked over to the truck.

"Roth, Caleb, like you to meet my nephew, Clay," Ethan called over.

The two men raised their heads and turned. As Ethan got closer, he could see an old car battery on the ground. Caleb was tightening down one of the cables on the post of the replacement.

Roth wiped his hands with a rag and stuck out his hand. "Please to meet you," he said and shook Clay's hand. Caleb raised his hand in a curt wave and slipped on the other battery cable connector.

Roth motioned to Ethan that they should leave Caleb to his work. The three walked over to the downed tree.

"Don't mind him," Roth apologized.

Ethan glanced over and saw Caleb slam the hood down and walk over to the driver's side. As he opened the door, an empty pint glass bottle fell out.

Clay pointed to a large stain in the road. "Uncle Ethan, look at that."

Ethan, Roth, and Clay walked over to a patch of blood-covered intestines, trodden in the dirt. A gory trail led into the trees.

"Damn things could have at least left something," Roth said.

"One of your hogs?" Ethan asked.

"Even tore up my cage."

Ethan looked over at the steel rung door, lying on the ground near the back bumper of the truck. "You know, I could probably fix that for you."

"I'd appreciate it. I got some cured gammon I could trade."

"Sounds good." Ethan looked over at the tree in the road. "Looks to be a cord or two. How about Clay and I cut that up, give you half, and you can toss in some salted rashers."

"Fair enough."

"So what happened? Was it a bear?"

"Caleb swears it was a pack of skunk apes."

"That so," Ethan said.

"You mean, like a bigfoot?" Clay asked.

"Folks around here believe in a lot of things," Rolf said.

"Maybe it's time to get Caleb off of the juice," Ethan said.

"I keep trying, but the man's possessed."

"My money it's a rogue bear."

"Well, then, we better stay vigilante. I can't afford losing any more of my stock. Be seeing you," Roth said and walked over to the truck where Caleb was waiting.

Ethan watched as Caleb started up the truck, made a u-turn, and then drove off down the road.

"Clay, go fetch the chainsaw out of the back of my truck."

"Sure thing, Uncle Ethan."

Ethan watched his nephew scurry over to the Scout. He went to examine the fallen tree. It was a red cedar, a fine wood for chests and roof shingles. It seemed a shame to just cut it up for firewood. The twig-like leaves were a lush green, and by the looks of the thick branches, the tree was healthy.

He walked along its length to the base where the roots were encased in a large clump of dirt, which if the tree were uprighted, would fit precisely in the three-foot-deep hole in the ground. A puzzled look came over his face as he kept staring down at the hole.

Clay came over, lugging the chainsaw. "Uncle Ethan. Something wrong?"

"This tree didn't fall on its own accord. Something shoved over."

5

Mia opened her eyes and saw the faint light on the frosted panes of the bedroom window. The cold air in the room chilled her face, and when she gasped and blew out a puff of air, she could see vapor coming out of her mouth. She glanced over and saw the covers drawn back next to her. She vaguely remembered Clay jumping out of bed to answer the door then coming back for his clothes and kissing her on the neck before hurrying out of the room.

Reluctantly, she kicked off the heavy blanket and swung her bare feet onto the floor. It was like stepping onto the frigid surface of an iced-over pond. She immediately snatched up a pair of thick socks and put them on.

She slipped on her robe and looked down at Casey. He looked cozy, fast asleep in his red sleeper pajamas and his matching red woolen cap, snuggled under his quilt.

Mia decided not to wake him just yet. He would need changing, but it was too cold to undress him. She certainly didn't want to start her day with Casey bawling, and decided that she had to find a way to warm the place up.

But first, she stepped into the small washroom just off the bedroom. She poured some water from a pitcher into a porcelain washbasin and splashed her face. After she dried her face, she sat down on the toilet seat resting on top of a five-gallon bucket and relieved herself. She removed the seat and put the lid on the bucket.

Mia stepped out of the bedroom, leaving the door opened just a crack in case Casey should wake up, and went into the kitchen area. She bent over and opened the cast-iron door on the wood-burning stove. There was a remnant of charred wood lying in five inches of gray ash.

A wooden crate was next to the stove with everything Mia would need to stoke up a new fire. Mia grabbed a hand trowel and scooped out the ash into a pail. Once she was done, she wadded up some paper and placed it inside. Next, she laid in two logs in one direction then placed two more on top in the other direction.

She found a box of stick matches, swiped the head of one on the rough igniter surface on the side of the box, and touched the flame to the paper. She looked up to make sure that the handle on the smokestack was turned up so as not to smoke out the cabin before closing the door.

Mia placed her hands in front of the stove, palms out, and could already feel the heat wafting off the cast-iron which served not only as a source of heating the cabin, it also had a cooking surface. There was the drawback that after considerable use, the air in the cabin would become too dry to breathe though there was a workaround.

She took a pot down from a shelf and went over to the sink. She worked the hand pump a few times to get the air out of the line before water started gurgling out in short gushes into the pot. She placed the pot of water on the cooking surface so that steam would later humidify the inside of the cabin.

Mia would have to keep a strict watch over Casey whenever he was crawling about and keep him away from the stove. She had visions of him standing, grabbing the pot handle, and pulling the scalding liquid down on him.

And where was the nearest hospital? Or doctor for that matter? What if Casey did hurt himself or got sick? Where would she take him? Not being able to answer those questions meant that she had to watch him like a hawk, every second, of every day.

But what choice did she have? If they hadn't gotten the offer from Clay's uncle, who knows where they would be. Her parents were spiteful zealots and kicked her out of the house once they learned she was pregnant. That's when she moved in with Clay and his mom.

Jobs were scarce and Clay could only find odd jobs and never steady work.

Once Casey was born, the Morgan home suddenly seemed too small with just a ten-pound addition. How much room did a baby need?

But then, as her grandmother used to say, things happened for a reason.

Clay's mom met someone that was halfway decent. One thing led to another, and before the dust could settle, they were talking about marriage. Clay never talked much about his father who stepped out on him and his mother and never came back, when Clay was only five years old.

Mia knew there was no way one more person could be living in that house.

That's when Clay's mom wrote her brother. Two weeks later, Clay's uncle sent a reply inviting Clay, Mia, and Casey to come stay with him.

And here they were.

There was still a lot to do, unpacking suitcases, finish offloading the car, setting up the playpen—even though she had to substitute a cushion for the missing section of vertical slats on one side—and the highchair, not to mention sprucing the place up.

Not that the cabin was neglected; it just needed a woman's touch.

She shuffled over to the fireplace and looked at the two carbine rifles hanging over the mantle. Four boxes of ammunition were on the shelf next to a faded photograph in a cheap frame.

It was a picture of Clay when he was just a boy, standing alongside his uncle, each sporting big grins as they showed off their bountiful stringers of fish.

They could have easily passed for father and son.

6

Ethan hefted the heavy chainsaw and went down one side of the tree, cutting off the branches from the trunk into loose piles. He went back and trimmed off the small limbs and twigs, instructing Clay to gather them up and toss them into the woods for compost. The large boughs were cut up for the wood-burning stove and stacked in the bed of the Scout truck.

They completed the process on the other side of the tree, which left the larger task of sectioning the tree trunk into rounds that would be split later for firewood.

Ethan started at the base, sawing through the trunk. After completing the cut, he moved up a couple feet, and set the rotating teeth onto the bark and worked the saw into the soft wood.

Clay's job was to push each section out and wheel it like a tire onto the shoulder of the road, forming two separate groups; one for Rolf, the other for Ethan.

Ethan switched off the motor and placed the chainsaw on the ground. He looked over at Clay, who was walking back, wiping his gloves together to remove some of the sticky sap.

"How about we take a little break?" Ethan said. "Care for some jerky?"

"Sure thing, Uncle Ethan."

Ethan went over to the truck and opened the door. He poured himself a cup of coffee from the thermos and grabbed the paper sack of pemmican. Sauntering over, he sat down on a stump, and offered Clay the sack.

"Thanks." Clay opened the bag, took out a long strip of dried venison and handed the sack back to his uncle.

"Smoked it myself," Ethan said proudly and drank some of the lukewarm coffee.

Clay held onto the end and put the salted meat between his teeth and bit down. He tugged and gnawed, and kept trying to chew the tough marinated meat, refusing to give in, like a persistent dog with a rawhide bone.

Ethan burst out laughing. "Son, you best suck on it, less you want to pull out a tooth."

"Oh," Clay said and let the end hang out of his mouth like a flatten stogy.

"So, how you holding up?"

"I'm okay," Clay replied, taking the jerky out of his mouth to give his jaw a rest.

"As you've probably noticed, we do things a little different around here."

"You mean what you did with Mr. Becker?"

Ethan nodded. "Folks in these parts don't have a lot of money. That's why most people barter. Most everyone has something worth trading."

"The only thing I got is my car," Clay said.

"You got two hands. Some people don't have the knack to fix a roof, put up a fence. I do. I can teach you."

"I'd really appreciate that, Uncle Ethan."

"Good. Because I have another job lined up. Shouldn't take long."

"Do you think Mia and Casey will be okay?"

"I don't see why not. Blu's there and the cabin's well stocked."

The road was cleared and there was nothing more for them to do but come back later and haul away the rounds to be split for firewood.

"But if you're worried, I can take you back and do the job on my own."

"No way, Uncle Ethan."

"All right then."

***

Mia stared at the clock on the mantle. It was a few minutes past noon which meant that Clay had been gone for more than six hours. She had spent the entire morning doing things around the cabin. Most of their clothes she had arranged in a bedroom dresser after unpacking the suitcases and the overflow of clean items that were in the laundry basket.

She'd nursed Casey and fed him a jar of baby food—yams and peas—that he didn't care for as most of it ended up on his bib or on the tray of his highchair. He was cranky as he was getting another tooth. She prayed he didn't get an ear infection, as she'd heard that usually happened whenever babies were teething.

But Mia, a young mother of eighteen, was doing her best. She had never felt close to her own mother as the woman was always scornful and never showed affection.

So even though raising Casey was a daunting and tiresome full-time endeavor, Mia wouldn't have wanted it any other way because now she had her very own family.

Clay, a man that she truly loved, and Casey, her beautiful baby boy, who she would protect with her very life.

After some coaxing, Mia finally got Casey to take a nap in his playpen. She decided it would be a good time to go outside and bring in whatever was left in the trunk of the car and get it done before Clay came home.

Home. It was hard to imagine.

Mia went over and opened the front door onto the porch.

Blu immediately sat up on his haunches to greet her.

"Well, hello."

Blu swished his tail in response.

"So, are you here to watch over us?"

The coonhound responded with a boisterous howl.

Mia raised a finger to her lips. "Quiet down. You'll wake up Casey." She walked out onto the porch and went down the steps. Blu followed a few steps behind.

Clay had parked the car twenty feet from the cabin near a patch of tall grass by the framed-in outdoor shower.

Mia reached into her jean pocket and took out the car keys. Not paying attention to what was in front of her as she walked, she searched for the trunk key on the ring.

Suddenly, a force bumped her and she staggered sideways.

Blu bolted passed her.

"Hey, why did you…?"

That's when she saw the viper coiled under the rear bumper of the Oldsmobile. She recognized the thick body covered with black crossbands on yellowish brown scales.

It was a timber rattlesnake. And its venom was deadly.

Blu stuck his head under the bumper and pawed at the snake.

"Blu! Leave that fool snake alone!"

She ran over, grabbed the dog by the collar, and yanked him back, just as the snake lunged...

Setting its fangs into the hard rubber of the rear tire. The snake's body lashed as it struggled to pull free.

Still holding onto Blu's collar, Mia inserted the key into the lock and opened the trunk. She reached inside, took out the L-shaped lug wrench, and with the beveled end used for popping off hubcaps, she stabbed the snake through the head.

She dropped the tire iron and decided to leave the dead snake where it was and let Clay dispose of it.

"Come on, Blu. We better go inside. I'll bet you're thirsty."

The canine howled and dashed up the porch steps into the cabin.

"Crazy dog," Mia said with a smile.

***

Ethan drove through a plot of rust-colored pastoral land to a single-story house not too far from the edge of the forest. A wraparound porch stretched around to the side yard.

"This is Alberta's place," Ethan said, stopping the truck and shutting off the engine. "I promised her I'd do a quick patch on her roof while she was visiting her sister."

He got out of the truck then reached behind the bench seat. He pulled out a tool belt and fastened it around his waist.

"How do we get up on the roof?" Clay asked.

"There's a ladder round back." Ethan unlocked the toolbox mounted behind the cab and lifted the lid. "Grab about five of those shingles and that box of roofing nails."

Clay stacked the composite squares and slipped them under his arm. He picked up the box of nails, which was half full.

They went up the steps and followed the porch around the side of the house.

"I don't hear the dogs. Alberta must have taken Samson and Beulah with her to Porterville."

"Those are Blu's parents?"

"That's right.

Ethan stopped short.

"What is it?" Clay asked.

Ethan pointed to a badly dented metal shed that looked like it had been run over by a boulder. The door was bashed in. Bags filled with dog food had been taken out and ripped to shreds, the nuggets strewn all over the ground next to an open gate of a cyclone fenced-in kennel.

"Clay, go fetch my gun."

The young man put the shingles and the box of nails on the deck and dashed to the truck. He came back and handed Ethan his rifle.

Ethan ejected the 4-round magazine to make sure it was full and rammed it back inside the forestock. Pulling up the bolt handle, he slid the bolt back, raising a bullet into the breech. He threw the bolt forward, pushing the bullet into the chamber, and flipped the bolt handle down.

As they stepped warily toward the rear of the house, Ethan and Clay witnessed more destruction.

Some of the railing had been torn down, the four-by-four posts snapped in two like matchsticks.

When they rounded the corner, Ethan stopped to cover his nose.

"Uncle Ethan, what's that god-awful smell?" Clay said, taking a step back.

The backdoor, what was left of it, was lying on the rear deck. As they approached, they saw that the wood around the doorjamb was splintered, and there were only the screw holes where the hinges were once anchored.

Ethan aimed his rifle and pointed the muzzle at the doorway.

Standing at the threshold, they could see the devastation to the kitchen. The cabinets had been ripped from the walls. Spilled flour dusted the floor along with mashed food cartons and shredded grain sacks.

The legs had been broken off the kitchen table, and the chairs were lying on their sides, one reduced to kindling like something with enormous strength had stomped the piece of furniture. The cooler had been upended, and what meat that was left behind, chewed and slobbered.

"Looks like we'll be here for a while," Ethan said. "I can't let Alberta come home to this."

"Ah, jeez," Clay said, pointing at the corner of the kitchen where a large animal suffering from diarrhea had left wet brown splats all over the floor, and then must have stepped in the runny feces as the scat was smeared all over the floor.

"There's a shovel by the shed."

Clay left to get the shovel.

Ethan stared at the foul crap on the floor. "Damn things."

7

It was an hour away from sundown when Ethan and Clay finished their noble attempt at restoring Alberta's home to some semblance of its original self. For five hours, they'd hauled out debris, swept, scrubbed the filth off the floor, and did repairs.

Ethan fabricated and affixed new legs to the kitchen table. He was able to hang one cabinet back on the wall though it was missing both of its doors.

No matter how much they tried, they could not get that damn smell out of the house. They figured eventually it would dissipate on its own.

Clay helped Ethan with demolishing the damaged porch. After rummaging in another shed, Ethan found some posts and two-by-fours that he used to rebuild parts of the railing. He told Clay that they would come back at a later time to finish the job and throw on some paint.

Ethan had gotten creative and taken an interior door—unfortunately, it was to Alberta's bedroom—and was able to use it to replace the kitchen door that had been torn off.

The metal shed was a total loss.

Ethan wrote a short note explaining what had happened, in the event that Alberta should decide to come home earlier than planned, and left the message with his chicken scratch on the kitchen table.

As Alberta wasn't due back for another few days, Ethan figured he might be able to do a few quick jobs in exchange for enough foodstuffs to restock some of her kitchen.

By the time they arrived back at the cabin, it was nightfall.

"I'd call that a full day, wouldn't you?" Ethan said as he shut off the truck's engine.

"Hope Mia was okay I was gone so long."

They got out of the truck. Clay was a little slow going up the steps to the porch.

"Still holding up?" Ethan commented, following behind.

"I'm all right."

As soon as Clay opened the cabin door, they were greeted with the wonderful aroma of stew, which was simmering in a large pot on the wood-burning stove. A crackling fire radiated warmth and cast an orange glow about the cabin's interior.

A lantern on the drain board provided ambient light on the small kitchen table where three bowls with spoons and cloth napkins were arranged on a checkered tablecloth.

Ethan and Clay stood amazed.

Mia stepped from the kitchen. She wiped her hands on the apron tied around her slim waist. "Hope you two are hungry?"

"You might say we worked up an appetite," Ethan said, giving Clay a wink. He shrugged out of his jacket and hung it on a hook on the wall as he closed the door.

"I could eat a horse," Clay proclaimed. He took off his coat and draped it over the back of the chair by the fire.

Ethan and Clay sat at the table and put their napkins on their laps. Mia took each bowl and filled it with hot stew. She brought over a basket of freshly baked biscuits, already buttered, and placed it in the middle of the table.

"I must say, Mia, this looks mighty good," Ethan said.

"Well, thank you, Uncle Ethan," Mia said, sitting down across from Clay. "It's okay if I call you Uncle Ethan?"

"Seem strange not to." Ethan smiled.

"So, how was your day?" Mia asked.

"Got that tree cut up and off the road," Ethan said. "Be splitting it up tomorrow."

"Clay?"

"Well..." Clay hesitated then glanced over at Ethan who was earnestly enjoying his stew to see the troubled look on his nephew's face.

Ethan soaked up the last of the broth in his bowl with a biscuit, stuffed it in his mouth, and sat back in his chair. "Mia, I have to say you're a fine cook. You might want to share that recipe with Alberta."

"So she can cook it for you?" Mia asked, smiling as she ate her supper.

"Now don't get me wrong. Alberta's a fine cook…it's just…" Ethan was getting a little flabbergasted.

"Now I get it," Clay said. "You're keen on her."

"Why do you say that?" Mia asked.

"Well, we were out at her place today and—"

"Clay," Ethan said abruptly. "There's no need to go into all that."

"Go into what?" Mia asked.

"We had to fix her house up a bit," Ethan said.

"A bit? You should have seen it, Mia. The place was destroyed."

"Did someone break in?"

"More like something." Clay turned to his uncle. "Tell her, Uncle Ethan."

"Clay, just let it go for now. Is that coffee I smell?"

"Sure is," Mia said and stood up, collecting the empty bowls. "Let me get you a cup."

"So where's Casey, in his crib?" Clay asked.

"Go see for yourself."

Ethan got up, walked over to the stone hearth and tossed another log onto the fire, creating a brief bright flash.

Clay went over and opened the bedroom door enough to peek inside. Blu was fast asleep on the bed, curled up beside Casey; the toddler snuggled in his red one-piece sleep pajamas with the sewed-on booties and his nightcap pulled down around his ears.

 Mia brought Ethan a mug of coffee which he drank standing by the fireplace. She went over and joined Clay, still watching his son sleeping peacefully.

"He's really something," Mia whispered.

"I know. He's our boy."

"True. But I was talking about Blu."

Clay gave Mia a questioning look.

"Before you go off with Uncle Ethan tomorrow, there's a dead rattler under our car."

"What?"

But before Mia could answer, Ethan came over and said in a low voice, "Blu, get up. Time to go."

The coonhound opened his eyes and lay there for a few seconds before budging then got up slowly so as not to disturb Casey. Blu stepped gingerly across the mattress, jumped down on the floor, and padded out of the room.

Ethan put his empty mug on the table and went over to the front door to retrieve his jacket off the wall hook.

"Thank you for the fine meal," he said to Mia.

"You're welcome."

"Clay, better get some rest. I'll be coming for you bright and early," Ethan said as he opened the front door, let Blu go first, and closed the door as he went out.

Casey began to cry from the other room.

"That boy. He's going to drain me dry," Mia said.

"Yeah, but he'll grow up to be big and strong."

"That so." Mia reached up and pinched his nipple through his shirt.

"Hey!"

"Be nice if you could pitch in."

"I don't think so." Clay yawned. "I'm going to sleep good tonight."

"You and me, both."

8

Caleb awoke from a drunken stupor and sat up in his bunk when he heard what sounded like a large animal howl. He was still in his grungy work clothes, the same sweat-stained shirt, and overalls stinking of pig. He felt around the floor in the dark. He found one mud-caked boot, put it on, then came across the other shoe and pulled that one on.

Pushing off the bunk, he staggered across the small converted feed shed that Rolf had provided for his hired hand, and opened the door to a moonlit nightscape.

From where he stood, he could see the outlines of Rolf's house and the barn, the dark spiky treetops against the less gloomy skyline, and the shadowy layout of the hog pens where most of the swine had bunched together.

He grabbed his double-barrel shotgun that was leaning against the wall by the door. Opening the breech, he made sure it was loaded with two 12-gauge cartridges, and snapped the gun closed. He grabbed some more shells and put them in his pocket.

As he stepped outside, he could feel the chill cut through his bones and was debating going back and getting his coat when he heard something moving around over by the barn.

He cocked back both hammers and walked toward the structure, listening for the slightest sound. As he got closer, he could see that one of the barn doors was open.

And then he heard a shuffling behind the door.

Caleb drew closer, raised the shotgun.

"Hold your fire."

"Rolf?" Caleb reset the hammers and broke open the choke so as not to accidentally shoot his boss.

Rolf stepped out of the barn. He was holding his Smith & Wesson .357 by his side. "Two of the sows are dead."

"So you heard it, too."

"I heard it. We better check the pens."

They kept a watchful eye on the woods as they started across the yard to the fifty pigs corralled together. An agitated boar brushed up against a large stag, shoving it into the fence. That created a disturbance amongst the other pigs as they let out harsh guttural whines, almost like they were throwing up, while the other wailing swine snorted and squealed.

Caleb and Rolf were too distracted by the clamoring pigs to hear the two dark figures coming out of the trees.

Each man was attacked mercilessly from behind and tackled to the ground.

Rolf was shoved facedown. He struggled to get up, but was pinned down and couldn't move.

He raised his revolver to shoot the thing on top of him. His arm was bent so far back that his elbow snapped and the gun fell out of his hand onto the dirt.

A powerful fist came down like a jackhammer and smashed in the back of his skull.

Caleb was flat on his back, and watched helplessly, as the fierce beast relentlessly mangled his boss.

He gazed up at the face of the creature straddling him.

Even in the dim moonlight, he could see its humanoid face shrouded with brown hair, the black-orbed eyes staring down. Its hot, fetid breath stunk worse than any hog wallow.

Caleb turned his head, and as the other monster, the black-furred one, got up and stood over Roth's mutilated body, another creature bellowed from the woods, summoning the beasts.

The massive brute that was bent over Caleb placed its huge hands on Caleb's chest, rolled its shoulders, and pushed down, collapsing his sternum and driving his splintering ribcage into his heart and lungs.

Caleb's last vision was of the two stooped hulks, lumbering by the hysterical pigs in the pens, as they disappeared into the woods.

9

Casey woke Mia up with his crying. This was surprising, as Clay was snoring like a locomotive chugging through a mountain pass. She climbed out of bed and threw on her bathrobe and slippers. The cabin was freezing.

Mia leaned over the crib. "You just hold on, and Mommy will see to you in a minute." She shuffled out of the bedroom and went to work, warming up the cabin. The fire in the hearth was still aglow with orange embers. She placed a couple logs in and used a small bellows to fan the embers into a rising flame that licked around the wood like an orange serpent.

She now had enough light to walk over to the kitchen. After pumping up the kerosene lamp, she lit the wick, illuminating a good portion of the interior. The wood-burning stove was still warm. She shoved more wood inside and stoked the flame under the cooking surface where a pot full of water was beginning to steam.

Mia went back into the bedroom and changed Casey, who was only wet. She bundled him back up in his red sleeper and nightcap, carried him into the kitchen, and placed him in his highchair. He continued to fuss, pawing at his ear.

"Here, suck on this," Mia said. She sat down at the kitchen table and gave Casey a teething ring that she had dabbed with drops of her own homeopathic remedy of boiron camilia. He immediately took to it and worked his cheeks to draw the soothing medicinal concoction into his gums.

Mia heard footfalls outside. She glanced over at the clock on the mantle. It was only just after four-thirty in the morning and wouldn't be light for another hour, so why was Uncle Ethan up so early? Surely they weren't going to work in the dark. Whatever the reason, she thought she better wake Clay up. Then she'd put on some coffee, maybe fix some breakfast for the two of them.

She looked at Casey. He was content, sucking on his pacifier.

Getting up from the table, she stepped over to the open bedroom door. "Clay, wake up. Uncle Ethan is here."

"What?"

"You better get up."

Clay sat up in bed and rubbed his eyes. "What time is it?"

"You don't want to know. I'm putting on some coffee."

"Coffee sounds good." He swung his legs over the side of the bed and reached for his clothes draped on the side of Casey's crib.

Mia walked over to the front door. She could hear a scratching on the other side of the wood. She was looking forward to seeing Blu, eternally grateful that Uncle Ethan thought enough about them to have his faithful dog stay and watch over them while he and Clay were away for the day.

"I'm coming." Mia unlocked the bolt and swung open the door.

The thing standing on the porch roared.

Mia jumped back and screamed.

"What the hell…?" Clay bolted out of the bedroom. He took one good look at the giant creature standing outside the doorway and raced for the Winchester lever-action hanging over the fireplace mantle. He yanked the rifle down off the stone face and ratcheted the lever. He raised the carbine, took aim, and pulled the trigger.

But nothing happened. The gun wasn't loaded. Clay reached for a box of ammunition.

The beast ducked its head and stomped into the cabin.

Mia backed into the kitchen, standing in front of Casey to protect her baby.

After clearing the doorway, the brown-furred creature stood erect. It was between seven and eight feet tall and had to weigh over six hundred pounds. At first glance, Mia thought it was a brown bear as it was covered with thick hair, but its upper torso and shoulders were not as round but more manlike.

Clay fumbled with the box of bullets, extracting a single cartridge to slip into the feed on the side plate.

"Hurry, Clay!" Mia shouted as she saw her husband struggling to load the weapon. Casey started screaming at the top of his lungs, frightened by the sudden intrusion.

The beast turned and moved toward her and Casey.

Mia reached down, picked up the boiling pot of water by the handle and tossed the scalding liquid into the creature's face. The animal howled, stepped back, and turned away.

Clay loaded the bullet and levered the Winchester.

The beast heard the noise and swung its arm blindly.

Clay tried to sidestep out of the way but was unable to avoid the powerful blow that sent him flying up against the stone hearth. Still conscious, he groaned, trying to get back on his feet.

Mia still held the pot by the handle. She swung with all her might and struck the monstrous beast on the back of its shoulder. "Get out of here!" she screamed.

Another creature burst into the cabin. It was gray and hunched over, almost moving on all fours. With a fast-galloped stride, the animal rammed into Mia, knocking her onto the floor. A large hand reached down and lifted Casey out of his highchair.

Tucking the boy under its arm, the beast loped out of the cabin, followed by the other creature. They thundered out onto the porch and clambered down the steps.

"They took Casey!" Mia shouted.

Clay scampered to his feet with the rifle in his hand.

Mia was out the door, leaping down the stairs.

"Casey!" She ran faster than she had ever run in her life. Her slippers fell off and she was barefoot, dashing over the rough ground. Sharp rocks cutting up the soles of her feet but nothing would stop her. The damn things had stolen her baby. It didn't matter that they were six times her size and could snap her like a twig; she was going to stop them no matter what.

They were already in the woods. She could hear them breaking through the brush, charging through the thick timber, they were getting away…

Mia was grabbed from behind and lifted off her feet.

10

Blu stood with his front paws on the window glass and growled at the night.

"What's gotten into you?" Ethan said, rolling over in bed.

The agitated dog began to scratch at the glass.

"Hey, stop that." Ethan sat up.

Blu let out a long, coonhound howl.

Ethan crawled across the bed, pushed Blu aside, and looked out the window.

It was pitch dark, but he could see the cabin below. A light was shining in the window and the front door was wide open. He could see shadows dancing about inside the cabin.

And then he heard a terrible roar.

"Jesus," he said and jumped out of bed. He didn't bother to get dress, ran into the front room, wearing only his long johns and socks, and grabbed his rifle. He threw open the trailer door and jumped down to the ground.

He jogged down the hill, careful not to slip and fall. Blu was right by his side as they raced toward the cabin.

Mia screamed.

He was fifty yards away, when two enormous figures lurched out of the cabin, shambled down the stairs, and stomped toward the woods.

Ethan was almost to the steps when Mia came racing out after the two intruders. Blu ran up the stairs just as Clay was coming out.

"They took Casey!" Clay yelled, stumbling onto the porch.

Ethan darted around the cabin and dashed into the trees. He could hear Mia up ahead, racing across the fallen leaves. He sprinted after her, almost tempted to lose the rifle awkwardly swinging by his side, but he knew that wouldn't be wise with what was up ahead.

It was when he was running between two thickly trunk trees that he finally caught up to Mia, and snatched her up off the ground.

***

"Put me down!" Mia yelled, struggling to worm herself out of Ethan's hooked arm. Once they were inside the cabin, Ethan finally released her. She tried to run for the door, but Ethan blocked her path.

"You're not going out there!"

"Dammit, get out of my way!"

"You'll never find them in the dark."

Mia looked over at Clay who was standing in the middle of the room, loading bullets one at a time into the Winchester.

"Uncle Ethan, we have to go after them. They took our son," Clay said.

"No one's going anywhere. Not yet," Ethan told them both.

"Then call the sheriff on the short wave so they can start a search."

"That's not going to happen."

Blu looked worried with everyone yelling and came over to sit next to Ethan.

"And why's that?" Mia asked with a venomous tone.

"What are you going to tell them?"

"The truth!" Clay said.

"And what is that?"

Clay and Mia looked at one another, not certain how to answer.

Then Mia finally said, "That bigfoot broke into our house and stole our baby."

Ethan gave her a wry grin. "Do you hear how crazy that sounds? You tell the authorities that, and the first people they are going to suspect are you two. Happens all the time. Any parent stupid enough to make up a cockamamie story like that, is usually guilty as sin."

"Maybe Uncle Ethan's right," Clay said to Mia.

"You know I'm right," Ethan said.

"So, what are we supposed to do?" Mia asked. "Sit here and do nothing?"

"I didn't say that. First light, I'm going up that mountain and find your boy."

"Well, I'm going with you," Clay said.

"Me, too," Mia chimed in.

"Not on your lives. You know how dangerous that mountain is?"

"It doesn't matter. That's our boy," Clay said.

"You can't stop us," Mia said, stepping over and standing next to Clay in a desperate show of solidarity.

Ethan hung his head and looked down at his dirty socks. "You have to prepare yourselves that Casey may already be dead. Those things are vicious."

"You knew about them?" Clay asked.

"I did." Ethan raised his head and looked at both Clay and Mia.

"Did you know this would happen?" Mia asked in disbelief.

"No, no. I never imagined, it's the God's truth," Ethan said, his eyes misty. "I would never have invited you to stay here if I thought there was any threat. They've always kept to themselves. Something must have happened to make them come down off the mountain."

"You know, Uncle Ethan, no matter what, we're going after them," Clay said adamantly.

"And you're not stopping us," Mia added.

"All right then," Ethan said in a resigning voice. "Looks like we're all going."

11

It was near daybreak when Ethan returned from the trailer, carrying a rucksack, and pushing open the cabin door with his shoulder as he came in. He was dressed in a heavy coat, a flannel shirt, trousers, and hiking boots, and wore a pair of leather gloves and a fur hat with earflaps. He dropped the pack by the door, let the strap of his gun slide off his shoulder, and leaned his hunting rifle against the wall.

Clay and Mia were already dressed. Blu sat in front of the fireplace watching everyone work.

Mia was in the kitchen, busily putting some food together, while Clay stuffed some clothes into a knapsack.

Ethan went over to the center of the room, stripped off the blanket covering the trunk. He knelt in front of the footlocker and inserted a key into the padlock. Opening the clasps, he raised the lid.

Inside the trunk was a collection of handguns and knives with some other things.

"Keep in mind that we're going to want to travel light. A change of clothes is fine. And plenty of socks," Ethan said.

Clay looked inside his rucksack and took out a shirt.

"Is this all right?" Mia asked, pointing to the foodstuff that she had compiled on the tabletop.

"Biscuits, corn cakes, dry food, no cans," Ethan said glancing over. "There's a canteen on the shelf you can fill."

Clay brought his bag over to the front door and put it on the floor. He grabbed another sack and went over to the kitchen. He held the bag open while Mia gathered the items off the table and stuffed them inside.

"We'll need something of Casey's for Blu," Ethan said.

Mia ran into the bedroom and came out with the baby blanket from Casey's crib.

"That'll do." Ethan rummaged inside the footlocker, deciding which weapon to bring.

Clay walked over and looked down at the assortment of firearms. "That's a regular arsenal, you have there."

"Never hurts to be prepared." Ethan grabbed a brown leather belt with a holster and pouches with magazine clips, and put it around his waist. He took a government issue Colt .45 out of the footlocker and slipped it in the holster. "Here, strap this on," Ethan said, and handed Clay a fixed blade knife in a leather sheath.

Ethan chose a hunting knife with a ten-inch blade for himself.

"Take this Remington thirty-eight."

Clay slipped the pistol into his coat pocket.

"What about me?" Mia asked.

"I wasn't sure you'd want a gun."

"I do know how to shoot," Mia replied, almost indignant.

Ethan searched through the locker and found a twenty-two-caliber pocket gun.

"It's small, but it should suit you just fine. If anything, the noise should scare them off." He handed Mia the five-shot pistol and a small box of bullets.

Mia took the gun and shells, and put them in her jacket pockets.

"You might want this as well," Ethan said and handed her a folding pocketknife.

Ethan grabbed a few boxes of ammunition to take along and gave them to Clay to put in one of the bags. He searched and found a few more items that he thought they would need: a first aid kit, two battery-operated headlamps, a flashlight, a roll of duct tape, a cord of rope, waterproof matches, two ponchos, a pair of binoculars, a coil of snare wire, a slingshot for killing birds, and a double-edged machete with the blade hooked at the top for cutting down overhead branches.

Ten minutes later, they were stepping out of the cabin, each wearing backpacks, Ethan and Clay carrying their rifles.

Ethan led the way around the cabin as they headed toward the edge of the forest that stretched up into the mountain.

Clay and Mia watched Ethan as he held Blu by the collar and dangled the baby blanket in front of the dog's snout. The coonhound sniffed the fabric and began to bay.

"Okay, boy. Go find Casey!" Ethan ordered and released Blu.

Ethan, Clay, and Mia raced after the dog into the woods.

12

Clay had no way of gauging how long they had been trudging through the woods as it was still dark even though the sun had risen on the other side of the mountain. His best guess would have been an hour though his body was telling him that it was much more like twice that amount of time. And they had just started.

The effort had been slow as there wasn't a path to follow, just Blu howling up ahead, squeezing through chokeberry bushes and seemingly impenetrable patches of briar with sharp, spiked thorns. And if that wasn't enough, the landscape had taken a gradual incline, enough to cause them to have to lean forward under the load of their backpacks as they made their way, sometimes having to place their hands on the ground so as to steady themselves and not slip and fall on their faces.

Having taken up the rear, Clay could hear his uncle's machete up ahead, whacking away, carving a crude trail that they could follow. Mia was in front of Clay and was doing her best to slog through the deep bed of leaves on the forest floor. The muddy earth below sucked and clung to the soles of their boots making each weighted step laborious with the clinging mire.

"I don't get it," Mia said, pulling her foot up to take another step. "There's no way they could have gotten through this."

"Blu seems to think they did," Clay said, placing his hand on Mia's back to give her a push to get her going.

"I think he's lost the scent."

"You could be right, though I think Uncle Ethan would know if he did."

Up ahead, in the thicket, Blu let out a yelp.

"What's going on?" Mia called up to Ethan.

"Stay close," Ethan replied.

Clay could see his uncle swinging the sharp machete, blazing a tunnel through the wall of thick brush, pushing in the direction of the whimpering dog. Mia and Clay hunkered behind Ethan as the big man stooped to forge through the dense barrier.

The thoroughfare was a gauntlet of jutting thorns and dagger-like branch tips, snagging their coats and scratching at their faces as they pressed on.

Finally, Clay saw his uncle stand erect as he came out of the undergrowth onto a small patch of flat ground where Blu was sitting, licking at the blood-oozing scrapes on his side.

"You poor thing," Mia said, taking off her backpack. She opened the top flap and took out a shirt. She applied pressure to the worst cut.

Ethan knelt beside his dog and kneaded the back of Blu's neck, which seemed to calm him. "You're no good to us all cut to ribbons," he said.

"I hate to say it, but is this even the way?" Mia asked.

Ethan glanced around before his eyes fixed on a small tuft of brown hair stuck on one of the outer twigs of a nearby shrub. He stood and went over to the bush. He retrieved the fur swath, came back, and handed the matted bit to Mia. She looked at it and put it up to her nose. "Ew, smells just like those things that were in the cabin," she said with disgust and threw the lump of hair on the ground.

"I'd say we're on the right track," Ethan said. He reached around to a side pocket on his pack and pulled out a ten-foot long leash. He clipped one end on Blu's dog collar. "This is going to slow us down some, but I can't take a chance Blu further injuring himself."

Satisfied that the bleeding had stopped, Mia folded her bloodstained shirt and stuffed it back in her pack.

Ethan pulled the baby blanket out of his coat pocket and waved it in front of Blu's nose. The dog immediately took off, towing Ethan with him up the sloping terrain of the thick forest.

***

They reached a point where they were forced to scale a steep section that stretched up to a leveler portion of the mountain.

Ethan looked up and assessed the thirty-foot incline of composite dirt and roots jutting out of the sheer earth. It looked more difficult than it was. There were plenty of roots that could be used for handholds, and the hillside was loose enough to drive the tips of their boots for decent footholds.

A few short-leaf pines were along the way, and a large fallen chestnut oak at the top that looked as though it had been there for decades as it was decayed and rotted into various-sized logs.

"Watch me as I go up and do what I do. Clay, you're going to have to bring my rifle and pack up as I'm going to have to carry Blu."

"Sure thing," Clay said.

Ethan slung the rifle off his shoulder and let his backpack drop to the ground.

"I can carry the rifle," Mia said.

"Come here, boy," Ethan said. He still had the end of the leash looped around his wrist. He picked Blu up, and held him around the rump so that the dog faced backward and could drape his front legs over Ethan's shoulder.

"You sure you can climb up like that?" Clay asked.

"Well, I certainly hope so," Ethan said. He reached up for the nearest root and pulled himself up, planting the toe of his boot into the dirt wall. He raised his other boot and stood on a bulbous knob. He pressed Blu's back against the embankment and used his free hand to grab a protruding root to anchor him as he reached up with his other hand for another grappling.

As Ethan continued up, both Clay and Mia looked on in amazement. Once Ethan was at the halfway mark, Mia started her ascent. Clay waited until she was a couple feet above his head before he followed.

After a few minutes, Ethan finally reached the bottom of the fallen tree. He lifted Blu up and turned him around. The dog got the jest and clambered up the rough bark onto a sectioned log. Ethan removed the leash from his wrist and tossed the leather tether up.

When Ethan grabbed a thick bough which slowly dislodged from under the log, he immediately realized he'd made a fateful mistake.

"Look out!" he yelled, having released the brake under the set log as it began to roll downward.

Blu barked and leapt backward off the rotating log.

Ethan slid feet first down the embankment as the log picked up speed, spinning after him.

"Get out of the way!" Ethan yelled, skidding toward the couple. He latched onto a low-hanging branch and swung himself against a tree trunk.

Clay reached up, grabbed Mia, and pulled her out of the path of the tumbling log as it careened down and flattened some saplings and crashed into a patch of blueberry shrubs.

It wasn't until a few minutes later when everyone was brushing themselves off and resting on flat ground near the gap where the hickory log had detached itself, that Ethan said, "That wasn't an accident."

"What do you mean?" Clay asked.

"That was a booby trap."

"Certainly those things couldn't…"

Ethan held up his hand. "It wasn't them. This was manmade."

"By who?"

"I think I have a good idea. From here on out, we're going to have to be extra careful."

13

Mason Payne knew what death warmed over felt like because that's the way he felt at the moment, sprawled on his sofa, his mind fogged from too much moonshine and weed from the night before. He looked like a big black bear in boxers, with his wooly beard, furry chest, and hair legs.

A white scar ran down the left side of his face from the middle of his forehead, intersecting with the black patch where his eye once resided, as it stretched over his cheek down into the tuff of his beard. It was the fine work of the paternal Payne, a demonic man that loved nothing better than to instill fear into his four sons. Mason's personal family brand had been by the jagged end of a broken whiskey bottle.

He opened his good eye and stared over at the coffee table cluttered with an overflowing glass ashtray filled with cigarette butts, bags of weed, his Ruger P85 nine-millimeter double-action automatic, a near-empty Mason jar of hooch, and a bunch of crumbled wrappers and sacks from a take-out diner, that at the moment, he couldn't quite remember the name of.

That's how wasted he was.

So he certainly wasn't in any condition to acknowledge the three strangers standing in his living room that were looking down at him like he was some kind of road kill that they couldn't quite identify.

"Looks like you came up a couple toes short playing 'this little piggy,'" said the sleaze with the prison tats on his neck, referring to the two missing toes on Mason's foot.

The interloper was standing on the other side of the coffee table, pointing the business end of a large bore riot gun.

Standing by the door, another scuzzbag holding a sawed-off shotgun by his hip let out a laugh like it was the best punch line he had heard in years.

The skinny guy in the long coat by the kitchen doorway didn't seem as amused and just stood stolid, pointing his pistol.

Mason pushed off the cushion and sat up, planting his bare feet on the sticky carpet. "So…what are you peckerwoods doing here?"

The skinny guy didn't find Mason humorous either. "You better shut your mouth or we'll do it for you."

"That right." Mason leaned forward to reach for his cigarettes, which were in equal distance of his handgun.

"I wouldn't if I were you."

"I just want a smoke."

The sleaze with the tats picked up the Zippo lighter and the pack of Marlboro lights and tossed them onto Mason's lap. "Think of it as your last request."

Mason plucked a cigarette out of the box, put it between his lips, flipped open the lighter, and ignited the tobacco tip with the first spin of the Zippo. He snapped the lighter closed. After taking a long drag, he let out a slow stream of smoke, and said, "Aren't you fellas on the wrong side of the mountain?"

"Not by where we stand. You're the one that's crossed over the line. No one does business in Porterville but us."

"From what I've heard, it's a free country. Man has a right to free enterprise."

"Not around here he doesn't," the skinny guy said, emphasizing with the wag of his gun. "If you haven't guessed by now, we're here to put you out of business. Permanently. Clive, you want to do the honors?"

Clive stepped away from the door, and sauntered across the room, all the while lifting his short barrel scattergun.

Mason tensed his muscles, shooting a sidewise glance at the Ruger on the coffee table.

A loud engine steadily approached outside which caught everyone's attention as tires crunched up the gravel driveway out front and came to a grinding stop.

The engine switched off.

Clive went over to the nearest window and peeked out the slit between the curtains. "It's Landon Payne and the other dipshit twin."

"Well, won't the boss love this? Looks like we're going to put the Payne brothers out of business, once and for all," the skinny guy said, and looked at Mason for some kind of reaction, but the man on the couch seemed as calm as could be.

Clive stood off to the side of the front door, aiming his shotgun shoulder-height to blast off the head of the first person to step inside.

The skinny guy aimed his gun, ready to fire on the next fool to enter.

The sleaze with the tats kept his muzzle pointed at Mason's chest.

Mason just sat there, staring at the front door.

Soon came a knock.

Mason didn't move.

Then came another knock.

"Why's he knocking?" the skinny guy asked Mason in a whisper.

Mason turned his head. "Because this is my house."

"Then tell him to come in."

Mason looked at the door but didn't say anything.

"Mason!" came a voice from outside.

"Yes," Mason answered.

"Get out here!"

"I'm not ready. You best come in," Mason shouted.

"Is the door latched?"

"Yes!"

There was a sudden blast and Clive was propelled across the room, a large smoking hole in the wall where he had been standing.

The front door kicked in.

The skinny guy fired at the open doorway.

A huge-framed man stepped out of the kitchen and shot the skinny guy in the back of the head.

The sleaze with the tats did the classic knee-jerk reaction and turned when he saw the skinny guy's brains splat out of the ragged hole in his forehead.

Mason grabbed his Ruger off the coffee table and shot the man holding the riot gun, five times, each shot drilling a gush of blood out of his body until he fell to the floor.

Landon Payne strolled into the front room. He was carrying an Ithaca Mag-10 Roadblocker pump shotgun. He looked stoic with his buzz cut and goatee, dressed in black like a Sunday preacher. He glanced over at the other twin, Jacob, who was standing just in the kitchen and was the spitting image of his brother.

"It appears our competition may have underestimated us."

***

Landon drove his El Dorado through the dust and up the quarry road. Mason sat on the passenger side, taking up more than his share of the seat. When the big man pushed back to adjust his legs, Landon thought for sure he was going to break the seat.

The cloud of dust expelling out from behind the rear tires of the truck up ahead began to thin out as they reached the stone ridge. Landon came alongside the old GMC long bed truck and parked.

Jacob climbed out of the cab. He was puffing on a cigarette that seemed like a white speck of food in his unruly beard and was a wonder that the burning tobacco didn't ignite his face. He leaned against the rear fender and looked around like it was the first time that he had ever been high up on the quarry's peak overlooking the polluted rust-colored lake below where a person could gaze for miles around and not see a single soul.

This was the case today.

Landon and Mason got out of the El Dorado and walked over to the truck.

"I hope they never decide to dredge this place," Jacob said.

"I'm sure they'd find their share of granddaddies down there," Landon said.

Jacob turned and tugged the tarpaulin off the bed of the truck, revealing the three dead men, lying on their backs, side by side, with their hands tied together.

Their necks and ankles were cinched with thick cord rope that was attached to heavy cinderblocks to weigh them down.

Jacob and Mason walked around to the truck's rear bumper and leaned their arms over the lip of the tailgate.

"You boys ready?" Landon asked.

"Ready when you are," Mason replied.

Landon reached into the truck's cab and released the emergency brake. He put one hand on the door's armrest and his other hand on the steering wheel. "Push!"

The twins put their shoulders into it and shoved the truck forward. The tires began to turn as the truck rolled to the quarry's edge.

Landon stepped away as the front bumper dipped and went over. The rest of the truck followed, plunging straight down the two-hundred-foot granite face. It entered the brown water with a thunderous splash, and after what seemed like nothing more than a minute, the truck gradually sunk.

The three Payne brothers continued to watch even after the truck was finally swallowed up.

Landon walked back to the El Dorado and got behind the wheel. Mason joined him up front while Jacob climbed in the back seat.

"After we go back to the house and clean up the mess, I want you two to pack up for a mountain run."

"Which one of us do you want to relieve James?" Mason asked.

"Don't matter."

Jacob leaned over the front seat and flipped open a sharp fold-up knife. He waved the blade in Mason's face. "What say we decide with a little mumblety-peg?"

Mason turned in his seat so that he could look at his brother with his good eye. He reached inside his coat and pulled out a pigsticker.

"Put those away," Landon said, steering down the steep side of the quarry, the big car hugging the road like a military tank. "I don't want you two laming each other. You know, on second thought, maybe we should make this our final run as we're going to need some quick cash. Sooner or later, they're going to come looking for those jokers at the bottom of the quarry. Means we're going to have to hide out for a while."

"Where to?" Mason asked.

"After we get James and harvest that crop, somewhere down south. I'll figure the logistics later."

The twins put away their knives and settled back in their seats as they headed back to the house for a major cleanup.

14

Finally bright daylight filtered down between the trees and the upward hike wasn't as dreary.

Ethan could hear warblers in the overhead branches, flittering between the leaves, searching for grubs and building their nests. Noisy blue jays flew about in the higher treetops with nothing better to do than to disrupt the natural order of things.

Ethan could smell the telltale aroma of pot as he climbed upon the crest of a slight plateau cut into the side of the mountain. He gazed at the impressive field with its rows upon rows of 10-foot tall marijuana plants that stretched back into the trees.

Blu sat by his feet and sneezed a few times, not fond of the distinctly strong odor, which was overwhelming his keen sense of smell.

Clay and Mia stepped onto the rim, and stood beside Ethan, also admiring the illegal crop of cannabis.

"That's a lot of weed," Clay said.

"That there's easily a million-dollar cash crop," Ethan said.

"Is it safe to be standing here?" Mia asked nervously. "I mean, don't drug-traffickers post guards with machineguns?"

Ethan shared Mia's concern and glanced around. "I don't see anyone, but that doesn't mean they're not around." He slung his hunting rifle off his shoulder.

Clay followed his uncle's lead and held the Winchester across his chest, at the ready.

Mia placed her hand inside her coat and closed her fingers around the butt of the pocket gun for reassurance even though the puny firearm would hardly be a fair match against a fully automatic assault rifle.

Ethan held onto Blu's leash to keep the dog in check and started walking across the furrowed rows of rich, organic dirt. A slight breeze blew out from the trees, fanning the tall budded stalks, like a prairie wind swaying the tops of a wheat field.

The sudden change around them only added to their unease.

Blu tugged at the taut leash as if sensing danger.

"What is it, Blu?" Ethan said to the dog.

The coonhound bayed a reply.

That's when Ethan saw the body lying on the ground. "Hold up a sec. Wait here."

Clay and Mia waited apprehensively while Ethan and Blu went ahead.

Ethan stared down at the dead man. The right side of his face was completely gone, which at first, looked like it had been shoved into the whirling blade of a meat cutter. But as he leaned closer, he saw that there were indentations around the savage wound left by an enormous bite impression.

A circle of dried blood surrounded the man's lower torso and the empty trouser leg. The right coat sleeve was bent back, the arm inside a compound break as the bone was sticking out.

An assault rifle with a banana clip was lying in the dirt not too far from the body.

Ethan studied what was left of the man's face and recognized who he was.

Reluctantly, Ethan waved Clay and Mia over. "I have to warn you, this is something you might not want to see."

Mia took one good look at the mutilated corpse and gasped, "Oh my God!" She turned away as if she might throw up.

"Did they do this?" Clay asked. He instantly started looking around as maybe those things were out there, watching them at this very moment.

"Well, it wasn't a bear. A bear would have torn into him to get to his internal organs. I don't see any claw marks," Ethan said. "Plus half of his face was bitten off with one bite."

"That's so disgusting," Mia said, once she had gathered her composure.

"Any idea who he might be?" Clay asked his uncle.

"One of the Payne brothers. James."

"The Payne brothers? Who are they?" Clay asked.

"A mean bunch. I'd say this is their weed-growing operation."

Blu got a whiff of something and bolted into the marijuana field, pulling the end of the leash from Ethan's wrist.

"Blu! Come back here!" Ethan rushed through the plants after the dog.

Clay and Mia stayed with the dead man, not knowing whether to follow or not.

Soon, Ethan returned with Blu at his heels. He was carrying a human leg with a boot on the foot.

"How did that get way out there?" Clay asked.

"Your guess is as good as mine," Ethan replied.

"So what do we do with the body? We can't just leave him lying here for the animals," Mia said.

"Mia's right," Clay said. "I really don't know anything about him, but it just doesn't seem right to just leave him out here."

"All right then. But you're going to have to give me a hand," Ethan said.

"Sure."

The men removed their backpacks and put down their rifles.

Ethan walked over to the mouth of the cave and laid the severed leg on the ground. He went back, and together, Clay and he each grabbed one of the dead man's wrists and pulled the corpse just inside the cave entrance.

"There, gather that tarp and we'll cover him up."

Clay pulled the tarpaulin over that was on the ground and covered the body.

Ethan looked at his pocket watch. "We still have plenty of daylight, so I suggest we keep going. That is unless you'd rather spend the night here inside the cave."

Mia looked at the long bulge tenting the tarp. "No way."

Without another word, Ethan and Clay strapped on their backpacks and picked up their rifles. Ethan grabbed Blu's leash and made an extra turn around his wrist for good measure.

"Let's go," he said, pointing to what looked like an old migratory path going up.

Instead of heading in that direction, Blu was persistent on returning to the field.

But after a stern reprimand, Blu relented, and led the way into the woods.

15

After almost two hours into their hike, Ethan was beginning to think that Blu had lost the scent as the coonhound was hesitant and would stop, sniffing the ground, then look one way then another indecisively. He let Blu get a good long whiff of Casey's baby blanket, but that just seemed to confuse the dog even further. Ethan figured with all the handling, even though he had been wearing gloves, the fabric had picked up other odors that were stronger than the smell of the little boy.

"What's wrong with him?" Clay asked, as the puzzled dog sat down on his haunches as if the whole ordeal was just too much and he needed time to ruminate.

"He's having trouble picking up the trail," Ethan said.

"So what now?" Mia asked impatiently. "We should just keep going, right?"

"Give him a minute. You have to believe me when I say this is a big mountain. We can't afford to be off-track. Not if we're to find Casey."

"Maybe we should take a five-minute break," Clay said, looking over at Mia.

"I could rest my feet," she said.

Ethan looked up through the trees and saw a rocky ledge above. A stone face, void of any vegetation, rose thirty feet above into more forest. "We'll rest up there," he said, and pointed to the spot.

Ethan held onto Blu's leash as the two ambled up the crude trail.

Clay and Mia followed ten feet away, Mia just a step behind Clay.

"What if we lose them?" Mia whispered to Clay. "What then?"

Clay glanced over his shoulder. "Mia, we're going to find him. You have to believe that."

"How do we know he's not already dead?" Mia said, unable to stop the tears from welling up and streaming down her cheeks.

"Mia, we'll find him," Clay assured her and stopped to give her a hug.

They held each other for a moment, and that seemed to be what Mia needed to muster her courage. "I'll be all right. We better catch up."

Clay kissed Mia on the cheek and turned. They were almost to the ledge, stepping out of the trees...

When a watermelon-size rock struck the granite and bounced off the ground like a cannonball right for Clay and Mia. They dove out of the way just in time, avoiding the rock as it smashed into the brush behind them.

Another rock hailed down from above.

"Find some cover!" Ethan yelled. He scrambled behind a tree stump with Blu.

Ethan stole a peek and saw the two looming figures on the ridge above. They were bending over, picking up stones, and throwing them down like contestants at a carnival, attempting to strike down targets, not for prizes but to draw blood.

The black-furred beast roared as it picked up a large boulder, held it over its head, and then hurled it down. When it hit, the boulder broke into flying shards.

Clay threw himself over Mia as the rock chips flew over them.

The barrage continued, some of the well-placed throws almost hitting Clay and Mia, as the rocks ricocheted and hurtled over their heads.

Ethan raised his rifle and aimed for the next one to show itself.

The brown bigfoot stood with its arm cocked, ready to throw.

Ethan put the creature in his sights, slipped his finger in the trigger guard...

Blu yelped as a cobblestone struck where the dog was hunched behind the tree stump.

Swinging the muzzle of his gun, Ethan saw the black bigfoot howl triumphantly having struck its intended target and inflicting pain. Ethan fired off a shot, but knew it would never find its mark as the big creature had already stepped back away from the edge of the precipice.

Ethan dropped his rifle and scooted over to Blu.

The dog was on his side with his tongue hanging out the side of his mouth. His pupils were rolling back exhibiting the whites of his eyes.

His body started to shake.

"Blu, please don't die on me," Ethan pleaded.

16

Ethan discovered the narrow path that led up to the ridge where the bigfoot had staged their attack. He poked his head up for a quick look around to make sure they had gone before climbing up on the jutting ledge that had served as a battlement for the creatures. They had even amassed a small pile of cobblestones.

Clay came up and joined Ethan, who was standing looking at the loose stack of rocks on the ground.

"Did they do that?" Clay said.

"I believe they did," Ethan answered.

"You mean they're that smart?"

"Enough to set an ambush and pitch rocks. I'd say we were pretty lucky…" then Ethan stopped as a lump formed in his throat.

Clay pointed the Winchester as he scanned the edge of the forest. Even standing on the outcropping of rock, it was impossible to see further up the mountain due to the tall pines which allowed only a glimpse of the patchy clouds in the sky.

"Let's go back down," Ethan said.

They shuffled down the declivity to the flat rock down below and joined Mia, knelt beside Blu. The dog's front legs were stretched out while his hind legs were bent and pulled into his groin. His body did an involuntary jerk, went completely still for a moment then shook once again. His eyes were dull and he looked somewhat incoherent.

"How's he doing?" Ethan asked. He knelt on the ground next to Mia. He undid the end clasp on the leash hooked to Blu's collar.

"The seizures are not as frequent."

"We'll give him a few minutes," Ethan said.

"I thought for sure he'd been hit by a rock," Clay said.

Mia stroked the back of Blu's neck while Ethan kneaded his flank to soothe the ailing coonhound.

"Let's pray he comes back himself," Ethan said.

"What do you mean?" Mia asked.

"After he had his last epileptic seizure, he was temporarily blind for an hour or so."

"Poor thing," Mia said.

"The longer we wait here, the further away those things are going to get," Clay said.

"I know, son," Ethan said.

Mia glared at Clay. "I didn't tell you before, Clay, but Blu saved my life."

"What? When?"

"You remember that rattler I said was under our car?"

"Ah, yeah. What was that about?"

"It would have bit me if Blu hadn't nudged me out of the way."

Clay dropped to his knees beside Mia. "I didn't know. I'm sorry, I must have sounded pretty callous just then." He put his hand on Blu and stroked his fur.

After a few more minutes, Blu began to act his normal self, and even sat up.

Ethan poured some water from his canteen into a small dish he had gotten out of his backpack.

Blu slowly lapped up the water.

Everyone gave the revived dog a pat.

Getting on his feet, Blu's legs were wobbly at first, but then after walking about, he seemed fine in getting around.

"All right then. Time to go," Ethan said.

As they headed up the incline, Mia asked, "Did you see any sign that the gray one was up there?"

"No. And during the attack, I only saw the black one and the brown one," Ethan replied.

"They looked like males. Wouldn't you say?" Clay asked his uncle.

"The way they acted, I'd have to agree."

Blu bolted up the slope and was the first one at the top. He let out a boisterous bark as if to hurry everyone along.

"Looks like Blu's good as new," Clay said.

Blu bayed and ran for the trees.

"Certainly would seem that way," Ethan said, with a big smile as he led the others into the forest.

17

It was close to nightfall when Ethan said they should make camp. They found a small clearing suitable enough and slung off their backpacks. Ethan instructed Clay to make a fire pit surrounded by rocks. Mia was to gather up as much wood as she could find before it got dark.

Ethan went about erecting a lean-to out of large branches that would give them proper shelter and help contain some of the warmth from the fire. As they didn't have sleeping bags, they would be sleeping in their clothes and bundled up under a single blanket that Ethan had brought along.

The rear of the shelter was butt up against a small embankment, which served as both a windbreak and fortification. That meant that they could sleep in shifts and only have to worry about the semicircle of woods in front of them in the event of a night attack, which Ethan doubted would happen. He was pretty sure that the creatures wanted nothing more than to distance themselves as much as possible.

After Clay had built a fire, everyone clustered around, staring into the flames.

Blu nestled up beside Ethan. Clay and Mia sat together with their legs crossed, rubbing their hands in front of the warm fire.

Other than the crackling fire, the woods around them seemed eerily quiet.

"It seems so strange not having our baby," Mia said.

Clay put his arm around Mia and pulled her against him.

"I know. I miss him, too."

Mia looked across the flickering fire at Ethan, who seemed transfixed in another world.

"Uncle Ethan?"

After a moment, Ethan answered, "Yes?"

"Tell us about them. The bigfoot."

Ethan sat for a moment as if he had been asked to reveal a long-kept secret that once exposed would bring everything crashing down.

"I was hunting one year," Ethan started. "Up on this mountain. I'd been up here for most of the day and hadn't seen one buck, which I thought was odd as it was the mating season." He paused to throw some more wood onto the fire.

"I was coming back down when I heard what sounded like a large animal, huffing and moving about. As I got closer, I could see this massive creature bent over a deer. It was tearing the deer apart with its bare hands and eating it. At first, I thought it was a bear. But as I watched, I suddenly realized it wasn't. This thing was nothing like I had ever seen before."

"Did you shoot it?" Clay asked.

"No. I just watched it eat the deer. It was like I was in a trance."

"Weren't you afraid that it would come for you?" Mia asked.

"I don't know what I thought," Ethan replied.

"So what happened?" Clay asked.

"It must have gotten its full and went off because before I knew it, I was standing there, all by myself, staring at that dead deer, what was left of it."

"And you never told anyone?"

"Who would have believed me?"

"We would have," Mia said.

18

It was late morning by the time the Payne brothers made it up the mountain to their grow-site. Landon was the first to enter the field, and the first one to see the footprints everywhere and the bloodstained dirt.

"Something's not right here," he said, raising his arm.

Mason and Jacob stood fast, a few feet behind their eldest brother.

"What is it?" Jacob said, raising his pump shotgun.

"Looks like we might have been raided," Landon answered, drawing his Smith and Wesson .44 Magnum out of the shoulder holster.

Mason came up and stood beside Landon. The twin was well armed with a Colt AR-15 machinegun.

"Look how the ground has been trampled," Landon said, pointing to the impressions in the loose soil.

"You don't think it was them?" Mason asked.

"I don't know. Where's James?" Landon looked around and yelled out, "James! Where the hell are you?"

There was no answer.

"You don't think he's still asleep?" Mason asked.

"Not James," Jacob said, joining his brothers. "The kid's always up before sunrise."

"Then, where is he?" Landon asked.

They strode across the furrowed marihuana rows, pointing their guns this way and that, half expecting to be fired upon.

Landon looked inside the cave and saw the bulged tarpaulin on the ground. He walked over, reached down, and pulled the canvas tarp away.

"Holy shit!" Mason said once he saw his dead brother.

"What the hell?" was all Jacob could say.

Landon just stared for a moment, then said, "Look what those bastards did to him."

"Jesus, they cut off his leg," Mason said.

"And shot off his face," Jacob added.

"He didn't deserve this." Of all the brothers, James had been the innocent one.

Sure, Landon had involved him their business, but he had never made James, the youngest, do anything illegal other than mind the fields. And for him to have his life cut short for no other reason than to be watching over a bunch of stupid pot plants; it was enough to drive Landon insane with rage.

"I swear, when I find whoever did this, I'm going to…" but then he turned away, so that his other brothers wouldn't see his face, his pain, the tears.

"What do we do?" Mason asked.

"We should give our brother a grand send off," Jacob replied.

"And bury him," Landon said.

"Up here?" Mason asked.

"Where else? It's not like we can bring him down and have a proper funeral."

"No, I guess not."

"You know, there should be a couple jars of hooch in the cave," Jacob said. "I doubt if James touched it."

"Go get it," Landon told Jacob.

The twin entered the cave, and after a short search, came back holding two glass jars filled with a clear liquid. He handed one jar to his oldest brother. Landon unscrewed the cap and took a deep swig of moonshine. His eyes glazed over as the 200-proof alcohol jolted his system. "That's mighty fine," he gasped.

They drank and passed the glass jars around. It didn't take long before the three of them were slurring and having trouble staying on their feet.

Landon finally sat down in James' lawn chair.

Mason slipped inside the cave and came back out dragging two other folded lawn chairs. He handed one to Jacob. They set them up and sat down, almost splitting out the seats and collapsing the chairs with their great weight.

"You two ever wonder about our old man?" Landon asked.

"I know he was a no-count drunk that liked to beat on us," Mason said, taking a swig of high-octane whiskey and passing it on.

"I remember the time he whaled on James," Jacob said.

"You do?"

"Sure do, Landon. I thought he was going to kill James. That is, until you stepped in."

"I think we had all had enough by then."

"Shame it didn't end long before that, then I wouldn't be wearing this patch," Mason said.

"Sorry that I didn't step in sooner," Landon apologized.

"That's all right. At least you did."

"So what did you say to him, that night you interfered?" Jacob asked.

"Well, once I hit the old man across the face with my fist, I told him he should never raise a hand to us. When he gave me guff, I said that he had to sleep sometime. Told him how handy I was with an ax."

"And that's the night he ran off," Mason said.

"That was the night. After that, I swore no one was going to intimidate the Payne brothers ever again. No one!"

"You know what? I'm feeling a little…" Jacob was saying when his chair suddenly buckled, and the big man went sprawling on the ground.

Landon started laughing, then Mason busted up, and finally Jacob joined in. Their revelry only lasted for a moment and then the somber reality of why they had gotten drunk in the first place set in and they were quiet.

A few minutes later, Jacob was passed out on the ground, and Mason had stumbled into the cave to lie down on the inflatable mattress.

Landon sat in the lawn chair, staring at the million-dollar pot field, wondering if it was all really worth it.

***

It was early afternoon when Landon decided it was time to wake up the twins. He gave Jacob a swift kick in the boot, jarring the man awake.

"What?"

"Get up," Landon said sternly. "We've got a full day ahead of us, what's left of it."

"What do you mean?"

"Before we go looking for the yokels that killed James, we need to do a quick harvest and bundle up the crop. That way, after we've gone over to the other side of the mountain and paid them a friendly visit, everything will be waiting when we come back this way."

"You mean now?" Jacob said, sitting up and holding his head like it was about to come off.

"You want to start picking or dig James' grave?"

"I'll pick."

"Good. Wake up Mason and tell him to bring two shovels."

Jacob got to his feet and shuffled into the cave. "Mason! Wake your ass up!"

Landon took off his coat and laid it across the back of the lawn chair. He rolled up his sleeves.

Mason came out of the cave, carrying two shovels by their handles and dragging the blades in the dirt. "We really doing this now?"

"I want to be done by sundown. That way, we rest up tonight, and in the morning, we'll hunt them down." Besides the tools, there was also a burlap bag socked away in the back of the cave in a crevasse. Inside were two Marlin lever-action carbines with scopes, half a dozen high-caliber handguns, and a few boxes of ammunition.

Landon took one of the shovels from Mason. He looked down at the footprints cutting across the field toward the edge of the forest. "Try and not to mess up those tracks."

"So where we digging?" Mason asked.

"See that oak over there?" Landon said, and pointed to a large tree with dense branches that were providing an abundance of shade.

"I think James would like that spot," Mason said.

"Well, like or not, that's where we're going to put him."

They went over to the base of the oak tree and started digging.

All the while, Jacob was out in the field, stripping off buds and dropping them in a picking sack draped in front of his waist. The sack was full so he trudged over to the cave where he had laid out a drop cloth. He bent forward and unsnapped the clip on the lower portion of the sack. The bottom opened up and the buds spilled out. He tucked the bottom of the sack up and connected the clip, and went back out into the field to harvest some more buds.

Once the hole was deep enough, Landon and Mason walked over to the cave, wrapped their dead brother up in the tarpaulin, and carried his body over to the freshly dug grave. Landon and Mason grabbed an end and lowered their family member into his place of interment.

"Should we say some words?" Mason asked.

"Let's cover him up first," Landon said. He pulled his shovel out of the mound of dirt and scooped a blade full of soil and tossed in down onto the canvas shroud.

They were halfway done filling the hole when Jacob shouted from the field, "Landon, you better get over and see this!"

"Can't it wait, we're almost done!" Landon yelled back.

"No, you got to see this!"

"Damn," Landon said, and threw down his shovel.

"Should I keep working?" Mason asked.

"No, take a break. Let's go see what's so important."

Landon and Mason traipsed through the field in the direction of Jacob who was standing in a row, looking down at something on the ground.

"What do you think it is?" Jacob asked, pointing at the dead animal curled up on the ground. The body was covered with gray fur, and the head was tucked into its chest in a fetal position.

"Bear cub?" Landon said.

"I've never seen a gray bear before," Mason said, bending down with his hands on his knees to get a closer look.

"That looks like blood," Jacob said, indicating the dried crimson on the animal's side.

"You think James shot it?" Mason asked.

"Be my guess," Landon said.

"Think maybe James killed the baby and the mother killed him?"

"That's a possibility. Roll it over so we can get a good look at it," Landon said.

Jacob hooked the top of his boot under the animal, lifted it up, and rolled it over onto its back.

"Holy shit, will you look at that," Mason said.

"That's certainly no bear cub," Jacob said.

Landon went down on one knee for a closer examination. The head was mostly covered with gray fur except for the face, which had brown, leathery skin. The lifeless eyes were still open, revealing glazed chocolate-colored pupils. Instead of the snout of a bear, the nose was flat with large nostrils. There was blood on the thick lips where it had bitten itself in a throe of pain.

The hands were furry, the palms the same brown, leathery color as the face. It had four fingers and an opposing thumb.

He looked at a foot, and saw that it had a rubbery, brown sole and five toes.

The creature seemed pitiful, lying in the dirt. It looked like a filthy, smirched-faced human infant dressed in a furry costume.

"This here's a baby bigfoot."

19

Clay and Mia had been so exhausted from the previous day's hike that Ethan had decided to let them sleep an hour after sunrise. Ethan started a fire and put on a pot of coffee. He rummaged through the bag that contained their short supply of provisions and divvied up three equal portions of biscuits and some pemmican strips.

After the couple finally woke and went off to a secluded spot to do their morning constitution, Ethan had their meager breakfast waiting for them. He gave Blu his own biscuit and some water.

They delved into the biscuits, and chewed on the jerky, washing the dry cakes down with steaming hot coffee.

Feeling somewhat rejuvenated, they packed up their gear and continued up the mountain. As Ethan had never been up this high, he had no idea what the elevation was, but if he had to guess, he would say they were somewhere around three thousand feet, maybe higher, as there was a fair amount of dead wood and pine litter as well as ericaceous shrubs with red berries and flowers under the pinewood canopy of trees.

The slope wasn't as extreme as it had been yesterday, and though it was still a steady climb, the trek seemed less grueling.

They had been hiking for the best part of two hours when Blu suddenly bolted ahead.

Ethan picked up the pace and hurried after Blu. Clay and Mia stepped it up and followed close behind. They could hear Blu running about in the bushes, barking excitedly every so often.

"What do you have, boy?" Ethan called out.

"Do you see him?" Clay asked, looking in the undergrowth.

"He's over there!" Mia said.

They hurried over to where Blu was standing. His head was down and he was sniffing Casey's red nightcap lying amongst the pine needles.

"Oh my God!" Mia shouted excitedly. She rushed over and picked up her son's cloth hat. She pressed it up to her nose and then pulled it away. "I thought it might still smell like him but it stinks." Even though the head warmer reeked, Mia still clutched it to her bosom.

"What do you think, Uncle Ethan?" Clay asked. "Think they could be close by?"

"I don't know. If they were, Blu wouldn't be acting so calm. No, I'm afraid they're long gone."

"But you can't be sure, right?" Mia spun around, looking in all directions. "I mean, if his hat is lying right here, then..." she glanced over and spotted what looked like a path covered with fallen pine needles. "There! I bet they went that way!" Still clutching Casey's nightcap, Mia darted for the trail.

"Mia, stop!" Ethan yelled after her.

Mia hadn't run more than a few steps when suddenly the ground under her erupted in a loud snap causing her to scream and fall flat on her face. "Oh God," she cried.

Ethan and Clay came running over.

"Don't move. Keep your foot still," Ethan told Mia.

"What is it?" she grimaced.

"You've stepped in a steel trap. You're lucky it wasn't for big game, or it would have taken off your foot," Ethan said.

"It damn well feels like it," Mia snapped back, sitting up with her leg bent but not moving her foot stuck in the powerful trap. The metal teeth had chomped into her leather boot.

"Hold still."

"Easy for you to say."

"Clay, hold her leg still while I pry the jaws apart," Ethan instructed his nephew.

"Don't worry, Mia. We'll get this off," Clay said and placed one hand on Mia's calf and the other on her knee.

Ethan gripped both sides of the metal jaws and began to pull them slowly apart.

"Get ready to raise her foot out when I say," Ethan told Clay. He widened the jaws some more then yelled, "Now!"

Clay pulled Mia's boot up clearing the bridge just as the jaws snapped back together.

"Oh, thank God," Mia said with relief even though by the look on her face she was still in a great deal of pain.

"Let's look at it," Clay said. He undid the knot on her bootlaces and carefully slid her foot out of the boot. Her sock was soaked with blood.

"Get her sock off. We're going to have to wrap it up," Ethan said.

Clay grabbed the top of the sock and gingerly pulled it down Mia's ankle and then off her foot. There were four evenly spaced puncture marks around the flesh just above her anklebone.

Ethan found the old shirt Mia had used when Blu had cut himself up in the briar and tore the garment into strips. He wrapped the first sheet around to staunch the bleeding then added another strip as a compress.

Clay went into Mia's backpack and took out a fresh pair of socks. He slowly slipped on one sock, then the other sock over that to give her some cushion for when she would have to try and walk on her injured foot.

"You're lucky it didn't hit the bone," Ethan said.

"Lucky or not, it still hurts like hell," Mia replied. She looked down at Casey's nightcap, still clutched in her hand, and began to sob. "Now, look what I've done. How are we going to catch up to them now?"

"Maybe you can walk on it," Clay said. He held onto Mia's arm and pulled her up on one foot. "Give it a try."

But as soon as Mia put weight on her injured foot, she immediately cried out in pain.

Clay looked over at his uncle, who was sniffing at the air as he looked up into the trees. "What is it, Uncle Ethan?"

"I smell wood smoke," Ethan said.

20

The small, rustic cabin looked as though it had sprouted out of the ground as a sapling and over a century's time had transformed into a shabby dwelling. The sagging roof was covered with a thick layer of brown pine needles, rotted pinecones, and dried tree limbs dangling from the eaves, a tinderbox begging to catch fire by the billowing smoke rising out of the stone chimney.

The log structure was covered with green moss and different shades of lichen.

A yellowish-tinted window looked like it was made of amber or some kind of resin and not glass. There was no overhang or front porch, just dirt and weeds.

The oak front door appeared solid with additional boards nailed on as a further fortification against interlopers.

Ethan stood twenty feet away from the cabin and cradled his rifle over the crook of his left arm. Blu sat by his feet and leaned against Ethan's leg as they both stared up at the tendrils of smoke drifting up through the overhanging branches of the tall trees.

"What do you think, Uncle Ethan?" Clay asked coming alongside, one arm around Mia's lower back as he helped her to hobble into the small clearing.

"Not sure. There's a good chance there's someone inside, but there's no way of knowing if they'll be receptive to visitors."

"There's only one way to find out," Clay said.

"I know, son. Just don't want to invite trouble."

"It won't hurt to ask? We need to get Mia off her feet."

"All right, then. I'll go ahead, you and Mia wait here. Take Blu's leash and keep him with you. I don't want him to start barking when I get to the door and whoever's inside decides to shoot."

Ethan handed Clay the end of the leash. Mia hopped over to a stump a few feet away and sat down.

"What should we do if they start shooting?" Clay asked.

"Duck out of sight."

"But what if you're in trouble?"

"Let's hope it doesn't come to that." Ethan raised his rifle off the crook of his arm and held the front stock, his other hand gripping the rear stock, a forefinger inside the trigger guard.

He ambled up to the cabin and stopped when he was right up to the door.

"Hello in there," he called out instead of knocking on the door with his fist, which if he were inside, he knew would have sounded more like a threat than a greeting.

No one answered.

"We have an injured woman with us. She stepped in a trap. We could use your help." Ethan heard a sound inside the cabin, like the legs of a chair being dragged across the floor.

"Door's open," a voice said firmly.

Ethan didn't know if it was a genuine invite or if he was being set up to walk into an ambuscade. Either way, he wouldn't know until he opened the door. He reached down and lifted the latch and slowly pushed the door inward.

The interior was gloomy as the fire in the hearth was only smoldering, puffing gray smoke up into the chimney. Ethan strained his eyes to get a layout of the shadowy interior and looked down at the planked flooring.

Three steps in, was an animal hide rug.

Ethan could hear someone wheezing, sitting back in the darkness.

"We mean you no trouble," Ethan said, hoping to reach some neutral ground. He knew he was a perfect target, standing in the open doorway with the sun at his back.

"What's your name?"

"Ethan. I'm here with my nephew. It's his wife that is hurt."

"You said she trod in a trap."

"That's right."

"Damn."

Ethan took a step forward.

"I wouldn't if I were you," the voice said.

"Will you help us?"

"Well, I guess I have to. That was one of my traps."

Ethan lowered his rifle and went to take another step.

"You better stop right there. You see that bear rug in front of you?"

Ethan looked down again at the floor. "Yes."

"Lift up the head, real slow."

Ethan leaned over and grabbed the head part and lifted it slowly off the floor.

A large bear trap was recessed in the floorboards about five inches so that the bear rug would be flat and the menacing device wouldn't be detected by anyone that was unwelcome, entering the cabin.

"Go ahead and pull back the rug. There's a steel rod just inside the door. You can trip the trap with that."

Ethan did as he was instructed and removed the rug. He took the long rod and held it over the trip plate and lowered it until the trap sprung with a loud snap.

"There's enough pressure there to take off a man's leg," the voice said.

"Can we come in?"

"One moment." There was the distinct sound of flint striking flint, and then a small flame ignited on the end of a spire of straw touching the tip of a candlewick.

The room brightened slightly and Ethan saw an old codger sitting behind a small crudely made table. A rifle and a handgun were lying on the tabletop within easy reach.

Ethan had once seen similar weapons in an old gunsmith catalogue but had never actually seen them for real.

"Is that a Henry rifle?"

"Sure is," the old-timer said. He had a long grisly gray beard and his shirt was so filthy that it was impossible to tell its true color. "This sixteen shooter used to belong to my great-granddaddy. Been handed down through the years and seen its share of fighting I would imagine. Best gun ever made."

Ethan glanced over at the revolver. "That's a Smith and Wesson Schofield."

"Looks like you know your guns. Right again. Designed by Paul Schofield himself. For all I know, it might even be the gun the poor bastard used to shoot himself after when the damn army tried to court martial him."

"I'm sorry. I didn't ask your name," Ethan said.

"Name's Micah. Been living on this mountain all my life."

"Please to meet you, Micah."

"Likewise, Ethan. Shouldn't you be asking that nephew of yours and his wife in?"

"Sure. And there's my dog," Ethan said, hoping it wasn't going to be a problem.

"Does he mind you?"

"Most of the time."

"Then you better bring him in. Don't want him wandering around outside."

"Why, do you have more traps?" Ethan asked.

"That and other things," Micah replied dryly.

21

Micah proved to be a hospitable host offering his bunk for Mia to lie down on so she could rest her foot, which was one of the few pieces of furniture in the cabin besides the roughly-hewn table, Micah's chair, a long bench and an old steamer trunk with canvas sides. Even though he didn't have much, he was more than willing to share whatever he had.

He told his guests how he lived off the land, trapping game and picking edible shrubs and berries. He fashioned his clothes from animal hides and used their fat to melt into candles and other purposes. There was a nearby stream for water.

"Well, I guess you wouldn't be laid up here, if it weren't for my trap," Micah said to Mia, his way of apologizing.

"It is your land," Mia said.

"No one holds a claim to this mountain, and certainly not me. Sooner or later, she takes back what is rightfully hers. Winters can be mighty fierce up here. I once saw a dead man frozen up in a tree. Stayed that way for a good three months before the first thaw."

"What was he doing stuck in a tree?" Clay asked, warming his hands after he'd piled more wood on the fire.

Micah didn't care to elaborate.

Ethan was sitting on the bench; Blu curled up by his feet. "So I take it you know this mountain pretty well."

"Better than most, I suppose," Micah said.

"You know," Ethan said. "I might just have some spare ammo for that sidearm of yours."

"That would be right nice of you. I was pressing my own bullets for a while, but then I run out of gunpowder."

"So, maybe you could help us out?" Ethan asked.

"How's that?"

"We're looking for our son," Mia said. "He was taken from us."

"By who?"

Mia didn't say. She looked away contemplating how to reply.

"It was bigfoot," Clay blurted out. "There were two of them. Maybe three."

"You don't say," Micah said but not in a scoffing tone. "You want me to help you find your boy?"

"That's right. Come with us."

"I don't think I can do that."

"Why not? They have our baby boy," Mia asked incredulously.

"You see that old bear trap in the middle of the room?"

Ethan, Clay, and Mia looked at the metal contraption.

"That's why." Micah got up awkwardly from the table for the first time since his guests had arrived. When he took one step, a heavy but hollow thud sounded on one of the planks on the floor.

Micah moved out from behind the table and stood in the candlelight.

"You see I don't get around as good as I used to." He patted his left thigh and directed everyone's attention to the brace strapped around his knee and the tapered wooden stomp where the rest of his leg should have been.

"You remember me talking about that man that froze in the tree?" He looked down at his peg leg. "This was the work of his trap. Well, my trap now. The minute he saw me lying on the ground and saw what he did, he tried hightailing, scampered up that tree thinking I wouldn't be able to shoot him. But I did. It was so cold I guess I'd just stopped bleeding. Crawled all the way back here thinking I was going to die. Guess I was just too ornery."

Mia and Clay exchanged solemn glances.

"We understand," Ethan said.

"All I said was I couldn't come with you," Micah said. "I didn't say I wouldn't help."

22

"This should help heal you up," Micah said as he sat on the edge of the bunk and applied a poultice around Mia's upper ankle. His calloused hands weren't the cleanest, but his touch was gentle, and the medicine seemed to dull the pain.

"What's in it?" Mia asked, always interested in learning new home remedies.

"Well, it's a concoction of mine. Sage and lavender, mostly."

Ethan and Clay sat on the bench and watched while Blu slept by their feet.

"So, Micah, it's true you've never been off this mountain?" Ethan asked.

"Never had a reason to leave," Micah replied, slathering more salve below Mia's shin. "Anything I needed, I could get up here. I didn't always live in this shanty. Had a place higher up in the mountain with my folks. After they passed on, I just kept to myself." He finished up and let Mia put her sock back on.

"Why did you leave and come here?" Clay asked.

"Moonshiners drove me out."

"How come?"

"Don't rightly know. Just a mean bunch, I suppose. You have to remember, back then I was little spryer than I am now."

"So you put up a fight," Ethan said.

"Oh, you better believe it. But I got tired of the killing and living in the woods. So I eventually made my way down and settled here. Built this place myself. I know it doesn't look like much, but it's home to us."

"You said *us*," Mia said.

"I did?" Micah replied with a worried look then continued on by saying in a reminiscing voice, "I imagine there's still a few moonshine stills up there, just rusting away. And then there were the silver strikes that never panned out, but it never stopped the fools from tunneling underground. Hell, this mountain's nothing but a maze of giant gopher holes."

"So you never tried your luck?" Clay asked.

"Oh, I gave it a whirl, but I came up bust. Even if I had found myself a vein, what would I have done with it? You know, back when folks were settling these parts, the Iroquois Indians used to call this Stoneclad Mountain."

"Why's that?" Mia asked.

"Well, the Stonecoats, as they were known, were these legendary giants that were made out of stone and lived up on the mountaintop. It was big magic for the tribes. The Cherokees also believed there were giants who were great hunters that lived up here. They called them *Tsul 'Kalu*, the sloping giant."

"Sounds to me they believed in bigfoot," Ethan said.

Micah ignored Ethan and went on by saying, "And then there're the little people."

"Was that also a Cherokee myth?" Clay asked.

"Just another one of their tales."

"So what are the little people? Dwarfs?" Clay asked.

"Well, as I've never really seen one, I couldn't rightly say. My daddy used to call them *brownies*. Said they looked like walking skeletons, and were only three-feet tall, but he could have been making it up."

A noise, like an upward clumping, sounded under the floorboards near the table.

"What was that?" Mia said, looking down at the floor.

Blu immediately got to his feet and started to growl.

Micah looked at Ethan. "You best hold Blu back."

Clay started to reach for his rifle leaning up against the wall.

"No guns," Micah said. "And no sudden noises."

Clay moved away from the wall and sat rigidly on the bench.

Everyone stared at the floor.

A square portion of the wood-planking floor rose slowly, revealing a well-concealed trapdoor. The lid opened all the way and laid flat on the floor. A dark figure pushed up out of the hole.

"Oh my God!" Mia gasped as everyone, but Micah, stared in disbelief.

"This is my friend," Micah said with a kind smile. "Alden."

23

Everyone's eyes were on Alden as he looked at the strangers staring at him. He seemed frozen, not sure if he should remain or jump back down into the hole from where he came.

"Alden," Micah said firmly.

Alden turned to the old man still sitting on the edge of the bunk. Micah let out a grunt and patted his chest, just below his left clavicle, with the palm of his right hand.

The bigfoot responded with a similar grunt and mimicked Micah's hand movement, and then in a hunched limp, he went over and squatted on the floor next to the bunk by Micah's feet.

Even in the poor candlelight, it was clear that his fur was gray, and he was uncharacteristically short for the legendary cryptid, just over five feet tall, the same height as Mia.

There was no mistaking his muscular build—all three hundred pounds of him—under all that hair. He kept his gaze down and didn't look at anyone directly.

"I named him Alden after my granddaddy which means 'old friend.'"

"You mean, he's your pet?" Mia asked in astonishment.

Micah laughed and placed his hand on Alden's shoulder. "Heaven's no. We're more companions. I found Alden caught in one of my traps when he was just a pup. Not sure how he ended up on his own. As you can see, he's not that big. I think he might have been an outcast."

"Maybe he was the runt of the litter," Clay said.

"He did look sickly when I found him. And yes, at first I did consider him as a pet, just like your dog there, Blu. But over time, we began to form a bond. Even though I did almost cripple him.

You saw him limp. Makes me sad to see that, but he doesn't seem to mind."

"So, he understands you when you talk to him?" Mia asked.

"It took us a long while. I'm really not sure if I was teaching him or if he was teaching me. We just started understanding each other," Micah said.

Alden looked up at Micah and patted his chest as he let out a low mewling sound.

Micah nodded his head and smiled. "Yes, they're friends," he said to Alden and responded likewise in both their body and verbal language.

"This is incredible," Clay said.

"I'll say," Ethan agreed.

Alden kept in a low crouch and moved toward Blu. The coonhound's hackles went up and he started to growl again, this time the rumble was deep in his chest, like at any moment he might lunge and snap at the approaching creature.

"Blu..." Ethan warned.

Alden's hand reached out.

Blu tugged tighter on the leash.

But then something remarkable happened, because the second Alden's hand came down to rest on the top of the dog's head, Blu suddenly went quiet and began wagging his tail.

"I never would have believed it," Clay said.

Ethan let go of the leash so that Blu could get closer to the bigfoot. The coonhound nuzzled Alden's side, then backed away and sneezed a few times.

"Bigfoot's musk is pretty strong," Micah said with a laugh.

Despite the bad smell, Blu got closer and went down on his belly with his front paws extended.

"Will you look at that," Ethan said. "Blu wants to play."

"Let them go outside," Micah said. "Alden can get pretty raucous."

Ethan got up from the bench, went over, and opened the cabin door. The late afternoon sun was fading.

"Out you two," Micah said.

Alden loped across the floor, giving the sprung trap in the middle of the room plenty of leeway, and jumped out the door. Blu spun his rump around and darted outdoors after his new playmate.

Micah looked at Mia. "Remember I told you I would help you find your son?"

"Yes."

"I might not be able to make the journey, but Alden can be your guide."

"But how will we communicate?"

"I'll teach you," Micah said.

24

While Ethan and Clay were outside watching Alden and Blu play together, Micah took the opportunity to sit with Mia and explain a few things before their first lesson.

"Don't think of it as commanding a dog," Micah instructed Mia. "You're going to have to be able to read what Alden does. You have to remember, he can sense things too, just like that coonhound of yours."

"Does he have his own language?"

"If you're asking if bigfoot speak to each other? That I wouldn't know. Though I would imagine they do. I think all animals do. But Alden was too young when I found him, so I doubt he ever did. Everything we do is a way we learned together."

"Do I use my voice or will I be doing hand signals?"

"Either one, sometimes both. I think we've come up with about thirty overall."

"And you think I'll be able to learn all of them?" Mia asked.

"Nah, and I'm sure you're going to forget some by morning," Micah said realistically. "The important part is, that Alden learns he can trust you."

"You don't think he would hurt us, do you?"

"Alden's a wild animal, there's no denying that. And I'll bet he's stronger than Ethan and Clay put together. But I've never seen him vicious in any way, at least not to me. Maybe to some other animal that crossed paths with him. That's because he trusts me. And I trust him. Do you know, through the years, I've taught him how to spear for fish and what plants to gather that we can eat that aren't poisonous? He knows how to set a trap and hunt with his hands. At night, he sits and makes these little noises to himself, and I swear he's singing. I know, it sounds a little crazy."

"No, Micah. It sounds amazing. It's almost like…"

"A proud father bragging on his son," Micah said with a smile. "Yes, I know."

***

After some coaxing, Ethan got Blu to lie down on the cabin floor. It only took a minute before Blu was fast asleep, exhausted from playing with Alden. Ethan went back outside to check on Clay.

Micah and Alden moved over to the bunk, where Micah sat on the thin mattress and Alden took a place on the floor. Mia pulled up a chair so that she could observe for when Micah took her through the different hand movements and sounds that he used to communicate with the bigfoot.

Before each exchange, Micah would explain the meaning so Mia could make a mental note and practice the gesture. Alden's complete attention was directed to Micah during their gesticulations like they were two deaf mutes having a pleasant conversation.

It wasn't until Micah and Alden started using vocal exchanges and Mia tried to replicate the sounds that Alden began to take more notice of the woman sitting only a few feet away in the candlelight.

"It's more of a gruff," Micah said, correcting Mia, who gave it another try and this time got some approval from Alden as he replied back with the same vocalization.

"Let's change places," Micah said. "So you and Alden can work together."

Mia got up from her chair and limped over to the bunk while Micah hobbled over and sat in her chair. "Aren't we a couple of sad sacks," Micah commented.

"The sun's almost down," Ethan said, walking in through the front door with Clay.

Ethan and Clay sat on the bench to watch Mia and Alden.

"Would you two care to see our mine?" Micah asked, afraid that the two men's presence might be a distraction.

"Is it nearby?" Clay asked.

"You're sitting on it."

"What? Oh, you mean it's down there?" Clay said, pointing at the trapdoor on the floor by the table.

"That's right," Micah said. "Go have a look."

Ethan rummaged in his backpack and took out the two battery-operated headlamp flashlights. He gave one set to Clay.

While Mia and Alden continued their session, Ethan went over and lifted up the trapdoor. He set the strap of the headlamp on his head. Clay put his on as well.

Wooden slats had been mounted on the hard-packed dirt to be used as a ladder, leading ten feet down to the tunnel floor.

Ethan went down first, then Clay. As soon as they were on the ground, they turned on their headlamps, took a few steps and looked around.

The ceiling of the tunnel that was directly under the cabin floor was braced with crudely cut timber, most of it rotted, and looked unstable, like it could come down at any minute.

Down one way, there was a fork in the tunnel. As they turned and shined their lights in another direction, they saw that passage split into three other routes. The sidewalls were sloughed off and pocked from erosion and seepage, not carved smooth by excavation.

They could hear numerous sounds of water dripping in the darkness.

Someone moved in the cabin above and the overhead support rafters creaked, raining dirt down on their heads.

"Looks like Micah kept himself pretty busy down here," Ethan said, shaking the dirt out of his hair.

"It's a regular maze."

"I suppose if you didn't know your way around, a person could get lost mighty quick," Ethan said.

"Think it's worth exploring?" Clay asked. "Maybe it leads to the outside. Would explain why Alden came in through the trap instead of coming in through the front door."

"It's not safe. We've seen enough."

"Uncle Ethan? Do you think we'll ever find him?"

Ethan gave Clay a solemn look.

"It's been two days. I don't see how…" Clay said, unable to contain his tears.

Ethan put his hand on his nephew's shoulder. "We'll find your son. You have my word. Now, let's get out of here before the place caves in."

25

The Payne brothers were up at sunrise, packing up their gear.

Jacob had made a good effort harvesting, as there was a decent amount of buds accumulated on the drop cloth, enough for more than a single run down the mountain.

He had only been able to trim about forty plants, which left well over a hundred fifty plants that still needed tending, idle money waiting to be spent. Landon and Mason hadn't bothered to help as they saw no point in over picking as it was better to preserve the buds on the plants as they had no idea what was going to happen in the near future.

Landon always joked that money didn't grow on trees, that it was marijuana that put the big bucks in a man's pocket.

Jacob gathered up food in the cave for his pack. He found a half-filled jar of moonshine and included that.

He went outside and found Landon standing at the edge of the field, staring pensively out at the crop. It was easy to distinguish which plants Jacob had trimmed, as there was only the greenery of the leaves on a portion of the ten-foot tall crop.

Landon wore a backpack and was holding one of the Marlin lever-actions equipped with a scope, which served as a good hunting rifle. The butt of his .45 caliber revolver faced forward in his shoulder holster.

Jacob picked up his Ithaca pump shotgun and joined his brother.

"How'd I do?" Jacob asked Landon, always seeking his older brother's approval.

"That should do us for a while," Landon replied.

That was enough to put a smile on Jacob's face.

Mason cut across the field and walked over. He was also wearing a rucksack and was carrying his Colt AR-15 machinegun. "I've spent some time studying those tracks."

"Let's hear it," Landon said.

"Well, I found three different sets of bootprints. One of them was pretty large. I also saw tracks left by a dog. And then there were a few footprints which I've never seen before that were even bigger."

"You think it could be one of them?" Jacob asked.

"The bigfoot? I reckon so," Mason confirmed.

"But we still don't know who killed James."

"It's not going to matter," Landon said.

"Why's that?"

"Because we're going to kill anyone, and anything, that gets in our way."

As Landon, Jacob, and Mason passed by the giant oak, each one glanced over at James' gravesite, knowing that their younger brother was buried under that mound of earth.

And his killer was up there somewhere on the mountain.

26

Micah stood by the open cabin door and watched the small group preparing to leave. Clay helped Mia with her pack. She adjusted the shoulder strap and walked in a tight circle.

"Is that too heavy for you?" Clay asked.

"No, I can manage."

"I see you're not limping," Micah said.

"Thanks to your poultice," Mia replied with a smile of gratitude.

Ethan already had on his backpack. He was armed with his holstered .45 caliber Colt, machete, and hunting rifle; Clay, the Winchester lever-action, his hunting knife, and the Remington thirty-eight; Mia, her .22 caliber pocket pistol and the folding pocket knife.

Even though Alden knew how to use tools, he did not carry a bludgeon or any other type of weapon.

Blu was eagerly pacing, sensing something was up as everyone bustled to get ready.

Because of his peg leg, Micah walked with a lurching gait as he went over to a nearby stump and sat down.

Ethan, Clay, Mia, and Alden gathered round to say goodbye.

"You still have a lot of mountain up there to cover," Micah said, trying to prepare them for what lie ahead. "Some of which I know about. Watch for swallow holes."

"What are swallow holes?" Mia asked.

"Holes in the ground that are so deep, they swallow you right up, and you're never seen again."

"You're kidding, right?" Clay asked.

"No, son, I'm dead serious. Now, long before you reach the summit, you might come across the ridge above the gorge. Stay away from the edge, whatever you do."

"Why, is it dangerous?" Ethan asked.

"I've heard tales of men who went down there, were never seen again," Micah replied.

"Don't tell me. Another one of those Indian legends," Clay scoffed.

"Believe me, you don't want to find out," Micah said.

"All right," Ethan said. "We'll stay clear of the gorge."

"Then this is it," Mia said, sad they had to leave.

"Godspeed. I pray you find your boy," Micah said.

"Thank you for everything." Mia gave the hermit a hug.

Ethan and Clay stepped over, and each, shook the man's calloused hand.

After an exchange of waves, the small party began up the trail.

Alden, Mia, and Blu were walking up ahead when Ethan looked over at Clay and nodded to the threesome a few yards away in front of them.

Clay watched the burly bigfoot ambling beside Mia with the spry coonhound prancing along at her side.

"Ever imagine you'd ever see such a sight?" Ethan said.

"No, sir. Not in a million years," Clay replied with a grin.

27

After hiking almost three hours, Ethan thought they should rest up for a spell when they reached a small glen with an overabundance of berry bushes clustered in the middle of the thick forest.

Alden immediately sauntered off toward a large berry patch.

Ethan and Clay dropped their backpacks on the ground next to a log while Blu paced around, sniffing the ground.

"I'll be right back," Mia said, shrugging out of her rucksack, already holding a small tube of toilet paper.

"Don't go far," Ethan cautioned.

"I won't," Mia replied over her shoulder as she stepped between two bare-leafed shrubs that were so thinned out that they offered no privacy whatsoever. So she continued on. When she thought she was far enough away so as not to draw attention to herself, she pulled down her trousers and underpants, squatted, and did her business.

It was when she was hiking up her pants that she heard something cry out in the bushes in the opposite direction from where she had left Ethan and Clay. She debated whether she should walk over and investigate or just return to the others.

And then she heard the cry again. A sound she had heard over and over, so many times in the past year. A cry she knew all too well.

It was Casey.

Her first impulse was to run through the bushes, rescue her baby boy, but she knew that would be reckless, as she had no idea what lay on the other side of the gnarly wall of briars where the sound had come from.

Mia got in a low crouch and crept as quietly as she could through the brush, doing her best not to rustle the branches too loudly and be heard. She edged over to the thick, thorny bushes, and so gently, pried the branches apart so she could see through to the other side.

The gray bigfoot was sitting on the ground in front of a tall patch of blackberry bushes, gathering up the tiny fruit and shoveling into its enormous mouth.

Seeing it this close—the incredible creature couldn't have been more than fifteen feet away—Mia was astounded by its size. Even in its current position, squat on the ground, she knew the animal had to be a least seven feet tall. She could only surmise, but it had to weigh close to five hundred pounds.

Though it was the same shade of gray as Alden, this bigfoot seemed lankier, and that's when Mia realized that this was a female.

The bigfoot mashed up the berries in her mouth and spat the juice into her rubbery palm. The animal shifted its weight to one side and turned slightly.

That's when Mia saw Casey, cradled in the bigfoot's other arm. He was no longer wearing his sleeper and was naked and filthy. His tiny fingers were clutching the long hairs on the bigfoot's bosom.

Casey opened his mouth eagerly and the bigfoot dribbled the fruit juice down from her palm. The purple liquid was all over his face and chest.

Mia's heart was pounding as her maternal instincts kicked in. Here she was, watching idly, as this monstrous creature was feeding her very own son, knowing that there was nothing she could do to stop it.

If she stepped out of the bushes and confronted the bigfoot, she would be putting her son at risk, which would most likely get her boy killed, and her along with him.

Her only choice of action was to sneak back and tell the others. Ethan would surely know what to do.

She turned to scoot away, and in doing so, snapped a branch.

The bigfoot turned to the sound. She glared at Mia hiding in the bushes.

Mia froze. Not because she suddenly found herself in a stare down with such a dangerous animal.

It was because Casey was suckling on the bigfoot's black nipple.

"Enough," Mia yelled and stomped out of the brush to reclaim her son.

28

Ethan and Clay were seated on the log, resting their feet. Clay had one of his boots off, and was massaging his tired foot.

Tearing off a piece of pemmican, Ethan handed the strip to Clay. Ethan ripped off another chunk and gave it to Blu sitting by his feet. The dog gobbled it up without even chewing once and swallowed it down.

"Thanks," Clay said, slipping the jerky into the side of his mouth to suck on like a plug of chewing tobacco.

They looked over at Alden, who was hunched down on his hindquarters by a raspberry patch about ten feet away. Even though his hands were the size of a catcher's mitt, there was a certain grace in the way he delicately plucked each berry individually with his fat fingers and popped it in his thick-lipped mouth.

His lower lip was reddening from the raspberry drool. Whenever he opened his mouth, the sight was a little off-putting, as the blood red on his tombstone teeth made him look more like a feasting carnivore.

"Do you think he eats meat?" Clay asked.

"Don't rightly know. Micah never mentioned it. Though I don't think Alden got that big eating twigs."

"No, I suppose not. How much do you think he weighs?"

"Three hundred, maybe more."

"Do you think he knows what we're saying?" Clay asked.

"Why don't you ask him yourself?"

"I don't really…"

Alden turned his head casually toward the men. He smacked his lips, let out a deep snort, and cocked his head a few times at the fruited bushes.

"Well, I'll be," Ethan said. "He's inviting us over to join him."

"Boy, I wish Mia was here to see this. What's keeping her so long?"

"Must still need her privacy," Ethan said.

"Maybe I should—"

Blu jumped up and bayed like a prison bloodhound that had just picked up the scent of an escapee. He took off in a fast gallop and disappeared up the trail.

Alden stood erect and gazed up at the mountain slope but stood his ground.

"What's gotten into Blu?" Clay asked.

"I don't know. I better go get him before he gets himself into trouble," Ethan said, gathering up his backpack and rifle.

"I'll wait here for Mia. We'll catch up."

"All right. Hopefully, Blu runs out of steam before he gets too far," Ethan said.

Clay watched his uncle hightail it up the trail after Blu.

He bent over, slipped his stocking foot inside his boot and tied up the laces. He stood up from the log and grabbed the Winchester.

"Mia!" Clay yelled. "We have to go!"

He waited for an answer, but there was none. He tried again with a similar result.

"We better see what's keeping her," Clay said to Alden then laughed to himself for thinking the creature could understand what he was saying.

The bigfoot grunted.

"Well, aren't you something," Clay said.

Clay tried to remember which way she had gone, and when he decided he was fairly certain, the two went off in search of Mia.

29

Mia started to question if she had done the right thing, stepping abruptly out from behind the brush, when the bigfoot snarled and clutched Casey tightly in a protective hold. She couldn't see her son's face as it was pressed into the animal's thick fur. Would the beast be so fearful of Mia to accidentally smother her surrogate son?

Taking a different tact, Mia dropped to the ground in a squatting position to show the animal that she wasn't going to come closer and that she wasn't a threat. Mia placed her hands on the ground, palms down.

The bigfoot coughed out a warning.

"I'm staying right here," Mia said.

Upon hearing his natural mother's voice, Casey turned his head, and Mia saw her baby boy's face. Even under all the dirt and grime, he was adorable.

Casey began to jabber like he often did whenever he was sitting in his playpen.

The bigfoot glanced away from Mia and gazed down at the human baby cradled in the crook of her massive, hairy arm.

Mia swore she saw the bigfoot's fierce facial features soften as her hazel eyes showed a hint of—what, was Mia losing her mind—a mother's loving attachment for her child.

And then a thought came to mind. What if she tried communicating with the animal? Like she did with Alden. Sure, she only knew a limited amount of hand gestures and sounds, but it was worth a try, even though Micah had told her that he had no idea if what he and Alden had developed was even in the realm of how other bigfoot conveyed their emotions or actions.

Mia raised her right arm up slowly and with the palm of her hand, patted her left shoulder in a show of friendship.

The female bigfoot huffed and seemed to be taking an interest in Mia's behavior.

"I don't want to hurt you," Mia said to the creature. "I just want my baby back."

Even though she swore she would remain strong, Mia couldn't hold back the tears. She stretched her hands out in front of her. "Please, give me back my son."

Casey was no longer blabbering as he was back to breastfeeding, which repulsed Mia.

The bigfoot gazed down at the nursing infant, then looked at Mia. At first, Mia truly believed that the creature was contemplating returning her son, but then she saw the bigfoot's eyes darting back and forth, searching for the nearest escape route.

Mia stood up and pleaded with the beast. "No, please—"

The brown, male bigfoot burst out of the bushes and charged Mia.

30

Mia screamed and fell back onto the ground as the giant beast ran at her. She crossed her arms in front of her face in a feeble attempt to ward off the attack, knowing she was about to die a gruesome death. She snapped her eyes closed, rolled over, and curled up in a ball.

The bigfoot roared and stomped over. Mia could feel its presence, as it stood over her, ready to strike. She heart raced as she thought of that poor man they had discovered back at that pot field, and how terrified he must have felt as he was being mauled and dismembered. And now she was about to suffer a similar fate, maybe even worse.

Mia heard fast approaching footfalls, and then a collision of bodies. She glanced up and saw that the brown bigfoot was no longer hovering over her but was a few feet away, wrestling on the ground with a gray-furred creature.

At first, Mia thought that the female had come to her defense, which meant that Casey would be unattended; giving her the chance she had been hoping for so that she could regain her son. But as she caught another glimpse of the two beasts battling, she realized that it was Alden that had come to her rescue, and not the female bigfoot.

Mia's heart sunk as she glanced around and realized that the female bigfoot was gone and had taken Casey. She got to her feet as the two bigfoot tousled on the ground only a few feet away.

The brown bigfoot was clearly the bigger foe, outweighing the smaller Alden by at least two hundred pounds. They grappled like a couple of Greco-Roman wrestlers, only they were using their teeth, doing their best to inflict lethal bite wounds.

Alden punched his opponent in the face, which didn't seem to faze the larger thick-skull animal. The brown bigfoot snarled and pummeled Alden on the chest.

The blows were starting to have some effect on the smaller adversary as Alden was struggling to break free and fend off the attack.

Mia looked around and saw a tree limb on the ground. She went over, picked it up, and wielding it like a bat, she ran over and clubbed the brown bigfoot on the back of the skull. The beast reared back and stepped off of Alden to face its newest opponent.

The bigfoot raised its fist to strike Mia.

A gunshot sounded, and the bigfoot yowled with pain as a hairy chunk of meat ripped out of its shoulder.

Clay came running through the bushes. He was levering another bullet into the chamber of the Winchester as he rushed in. But before he could get off another shot, the brown bigfoot was on him, striking him with a powerful blow that sent Clay wheeling backward. He hit the ground hard, losing his rifle.

Looking at its bloody shoulder, the brown bigfoot only seemed to get angrier and ran at Mia, who stepped back between the bushes, only to slip as her feet went out from under her and she fell flat on her stomach.

Suddenly, she was sliding down a steep embankment, riding down a chute filled with fallen leaves and mud with her hands out in front of her, her nails clawing into the wet earth in an attempt to slow down her descent but to no avail. She continued rocketing down, finally reaching the bottom but not before tumbling across the gravelly ground and striking her head on a rock, rendering her unconscious.

***

Clay sat up and pulled the .38 Remington out of his waistband but by then the brown bigfoot had run off into the woods. He slipped the gun back under his belt and picked up his rifle.

He went over to Alden. The bigfoot was covered with twigs and leaves from rolling around on the ground, fighting the other creature. He looked a little battered around the face as there was a cut above his right eye, and blood seeping out the corner of his mouth. He moved about stiffly like a defeated prizefighter that had just undergone a grueling twelve rounds.

Clay looked around for Mia but didn't see her anywhere.

Alden grunted and ambled between two bushes. Clay followed the bigfoot to the edge of an embankment that sloped sharply down about 100 feet to a rocky bottom.

"Oh, my God," he said, once he spotted Mia lying down there on what appeared to be a dried up riverbed. "How are we going to get down?"

Alden looked over at Clay, and as if to answer the man's question, stepped off the edge and fell back on his back onto the chute.

Clay watched the bigfoot slide down to the bottom and take a tumble before regaining his footing. "What the hell." Clay held the rifle across his chest and skidded down the chute.

He went all the way down and rolled out onto the pebbly ground. He scrambled to his feet and rushed over to Mia. Alden was crouched beside her and was poking her side with his fat forefinger.

"Mia, are you all right?" Clay asked, dropping to his knees. He gave her a gentle shake.

Mia slowly opened her eyes.

"Thank God," Clay said, leaning down and giving her a kiss on the lips.

Alden grunted a few times unable to contain his excitement.

"I saw him," Mia said faintly.

"Who?" Clay asked.

"I saw Casey. He's with a female bigfoot."

"Are you sure?"

"Clay, she was nursing our son, like it was her own."

"Oh my God, that's crazy."

Once Mia was back on her feet, Clay craned his neck and looked up at the steep canyon walls. It was one thing coming down the chute but it would be an impossible feat attempting to scale back up.

"This must be the gorge that Micah was talking about," Clay said.

"The one place he told us not to go," Mia said.

"I guess now we know why."

"And here we are, with no backpacks," Clay said, his voice resounding. "Stuck down here with no food or water."

Alden made a guttural sound, turned, and started ambling into the gulch.

"Where's he off to?"

"Maybe he knows a way out," Mia said.

"Let's hope so."

Clay and Mia followed behind Alden without question, like he was their personal guide for the day, taking them on a leisurely nature walk in the park.

31

Ethan knew by the intensity of Blu's barking that his dog had something cornered and wanted the world to know. He stepped up his pace and jogged up the trail, readying his rifle as he ran, making sure there was a cartridge set in the chamber in the event that he had to get off a quick shot.

But when he finally reached the spot where the enthusiastic dog was keeping his quarry at bay, Ethan immediately knew that he wasn't going to get a clear shot without running the risk of accidentally shooting Blu.

Blu was perched on a rock ledge almost eye level with the black bigfoot, its back pressed up against a granite wall. Spittle flew out of Blu's mouth as he snarled and snapped his teeth.

The bigfoot growled and took a swing at his tormentor, but Blu managed to dodge the blow, standing his ground as he growled back.

Ethan slipped his backpack off and laid down his rifle.

Even though the bigfoot stood well over eight feet tall, Ethan, too, was a big man at six-foot-five. He drew his forty-five and pulled out his machete. If this creature wanted a fight, he was more than obliged to give it one.

"Blu, back down," Ethan yelled.

The coonhound kept barking and taunting the bigfoot.

Ethan knew the dog couldn't hear him with all the noise it was making, so he started to advance, figuring if he got close enough, he could get a headshot and end it right there.

A forty-five-caliber slug could do considerable damage, especially when it entered the brainpan.

Again, Ethan called out to Blu to back away, but he might as well have been yelling at a tree and telling it to uproot itself.

He was ten feet away, about to pull back the hammer on his handgun when the bigfoot suddenly lunged, clipping Blu alongside his right flank and sending him flying off the rock ledge right into Ethan. The dog fell away and landed on the ground.

The powerful bigfoot plowed into Ethan, knocking his gun out of his hand, and driving him up against the rock wall. He still had the machete in his other hand, but he was unable to swing the blade because it was pinned between them. Instead, he tried stabbing the creature with the tool's hooked tip.

But that became impossible as the bigfoot pressed up against Ethan with the intent of crushing him with its massive weight. Ethan twisted the handle of the machete, which turned the double-edge blade. As the creature continued to push its body into Ethan, the blade between them began cutting through both their chests. The more the bigfoot leaned on Ethan, the deeper the blade dug into their flesh.

At some point, the bigfoot must have realized that there was something wrong with its tactic, as it should have been experiencing some degree of pain.

The bigfoot took a step back and glanced down at its once black-furred chest now covered with a crimson coat of blood, which suddenly infuriated the creature.

Ethan snatched his gun from the ground just as the bigfoot reached down. He aimed up and fired his gun at the enormous outstretched hand about to grab him.

The high-caliber bullet punched such a large damaging hole that Ethan could see right through the creature's hand.

The bigfoot howled, clutching its wounded hand. It lumbered out between the rocks and stomped off into the forest.

Ethan unzipped his jacket and opened his shirt. The gash across his chest wasn't as deep as he had originally feared as the material of the down coat and his thick flannel shirt had served as buffering pads against the sharp blade. He figured the bigfoot probably suffered more.

He watched as Blu limped over and sat down in the dirt.

"Looks like you and I took quite a little beating," Ethan said, and gave his dog a well-deserved pat on the head.

Blu stretched out on the ground.

"Yes, I agree. Let's just stay put and rest for a while," Ethan said, keeping one eye on the trail below, wondering how long they would have to wait before Clay, Mia, and Alden showed up.

32

They'd been hiking nonstop for the better part of five hours when Landon spotted the smoke lingering in the treetops. He'd given the signal to the twins to split up, as he didn't want them to be easy targets, walking up the trail in single-file formation like a family of ducks.

Landon stayed low and crept through the trees. He knelt behind a bush and peered between the branches at the shack in the small clearing. The source of the smoke was coming out of the chimney, which was a good indicator that someone was inside.

Seeing as they had followed the tracks up to this very spot, meant that whoever was in there, had to have crossed paths with James, one way or the other. And chances were, that very person could be his killer.

Landon looked to his left and saw Jacob, hiding behind the trunk of a tree. He turned and spotted Mason, who was close by.

"Mason!" Landon yelled.

The big man turned and looked over in Landon's direction.

"Go up to the door and get ready."

Mason nodded that he understood. He crept over to the shack and pointed the muzzle of his AR-15 at the door.

"Whoever's inside, come out!" Landon hollered.

There was no reply.

Landon signaled Mason and the man kicked in the door. It was difficult to see anything inside, as it was pitch dark. Landon moved from his position and joined Mason at the opposite side of the doorway.

Jacob had moved in closer and was knelt behind a stump, with his shotgun ready.

Landon glanced in quickly and moved his head back, expecting to be fired upon, but he wasn't.

"We know you're in there. We see your smoke."

Still, there was no answer.

Landon looked across the open doorway at Mason. "Go in, I'll cover you."

Mason didn't hesitate. He stepped right in.

And that's when Landon saw the bearskin rug just inside, directly where his brother was about to step.

"Stop!" Landon yelled.

Mason's boot hovered over the bearskin rug, and hung there for a second, before he retracted his step.

"Shit, bro," Mason said, giving Landon a puzzled look.

Landon saw a rock the size of a grapefruit on the ground and picked it up. He leaned in and tossed the rock onto the bearskin rug. The hide folded in two as the giant teeth of the bear trap snapped shut with a muffled clang.

"Jesus," Mason said. He triggered the machinegun and fired a steady burst into the dark interior.

Their ears were still ringing from the gunfire as the smoke cleared when a single gunshot flared in the darkness. Mason jolted backward as the slug ripped into his shoulder and knocked him outside, flat on his back.

Landon pointed his rifle in the doorway and levered off four quick shots. He dropped the rifle and drew his revolver out of his shoulder holster.

Jacob was already running over to help his brother. And he was also carrying something in his hand. A flaming Maltese cocktail made from a burning jar of moonshine.

"No, wait!" Landon yelled, but he was too late to stop Jacob as the man was already lobbing the incendiary through the open doorway.

Jacob reached down and started pulling Mason away from the shack. "I figured if you wanted them out, we should burn them out."

But all Landon could think of was their money crop down below. "You stupid fool. You know what you've done? You've gone and set fire to this entire mountain."

Jacob caught on real quick. "Ah, shit." He let go of Mason and ran over to Landon. "What do we do?"

But by then, the interior of the shack was engulfed in flames. The fire was so intense that the heat drove them back.

They watched the burning structure surrounded by pine trees, knowing that at any moment, the canopy would catch fire, and the entire forest would become an inferno.

33

Landon watched fretfully through the open doorway as the fire inside the shack lapped up the interior walls and the flames burned up through the roof, igniting the cover of dead pine needles. The single window had melted from the heat of the conflagration.

Even as the fiery blaze raged, he hadn't heard a single cry for mercy or a scream from inside the building, which he thought strange, but then maybe he had plugged the poor bastard and spared him from being roasted alive and suffering an excruciating death.

The entire roof was ablaze as the flames reached upward, searching for more fuel. Overhead, the low branches of the pine trees were like sacrificial totems.

Landon knew if the trees caught fire they would be in serious trouble, and most likely would be trapped with no way of escaping a wildfire, that once it spread, would surely turn into an unstoppable firestorm.

He backed away as the heat intensified.

There was a loud crackling.

The roof came down in a blazing heap of sparks and crashing embers as the four exterior walls collapsed inward.

The entire structure fell into a large pit as if the ground had suddenly opened up, and in a matter of only a few seconds, the fire was no more a threat than a campfire contained in a fire pit.

"Holy shit, did you see that?" Jacob yelled.

By then the tips of the flames were barely extending above ground level.

Landon wiped his brow, thankful that he no longer had to worry about a wildfire scorching the mountainside and eventually decimating their pot field.

He walked over to the twins.

Mason was sitting on a stump and had his coat and shirt off. Jacob was tending to the gunshot wound to his brother's right shoulder.

"You're lucky I'm not going to have to dig that out. Bullet went right through," Jacob said, wrapping the wound.

"Jacob's right. This must be your lucky day. If I hadn't said something, you would have stepped in that bear trap. I'm betting you would have lost more than a couple toes," Landon said.

"Like he needs to lose more toes," Jacob laughed.

"Shut up, Jacob," Mason said, glaring at his brother with his one eye. "I would have seen it if it weren't for my blindside."

"You going to be up for traveling?" Landon asked.

"It don't hurt that much," Mason said. He stood and let Jacob help him with his shirt. "I spotted some more tracks leading up that way," Mason said, pulling on his coat.

"Good, 'cause after just getting bushwhacked, I'm in a bit of a killing mood."

34

"Be careful you don't…" Mia tried to warn Clay, but it was already too late.

Clay's foot had slipped on the rock face and he was sliding down to the ground.

"This is the fifth spot I've tried to climb up. I doubt if a professional rock climber could get out of this place." Clay blew on his hands, scraped raw from yet another unexpected descent down the rock face.

Alden had only paused for a moment to watch Clay's failed attempt and continued on his ambling way.

Clay and Mia strolled after the bigfoot.

"Have you noticed?" Mia said.

"Noticed what?"

"Just look around, don't you see a difference?"

Clay had been too concerned, concentrating solely on how they might get out of the gorge, that he hadn't bothered paying attention to the drastic change in scenery. Now that he glanced about, he had to agree with Mia. The terrain around them was different.

There were no trees or shrubs in the gorge, only the wide gravelly riverbed that had to be two hundred feet wide. The rock cliffs on either side were sparsely covered with greenery and speckled with various brightly colored flowers.

Up ahead was a behemoth moss-covered stone arch, one hundred feet above their heads that spanned the entire gorge. A cascading waterfall could be seen higher up on the mountain.

Everything looked almost mystical.

"And there's something else," Mia said.

"What's that?" Clay asked.

"I haven't seen a single bird or animal."

"You know, you're right. Neither have I."

"Don't you think that's a little strange?"

Clay glanced over at Alden, who had stopped walking.

The bigfoot was gazing up at the edge of the ridge overlooking the gorge.

Clay looked up as well, as Alden curled his mouth and snarled.

"Whoa, what's gotten into him?" Clay said, sensing the fierceness of the animal only a few feet away.

"He thinks we're in danger," Mia said.

35

Mason was on point, so he was the first one to see the two backpacks lying in the glen. "Hey, I found something," he yelled back over his shoulder to Landon and Jacob coming up the trail.

He walked over to the abandoned packs and waited for his brothers.

"Well, what do we have here?" Landon said, dropping to one knee to inspect one of the bags. He untied the flap and opened the pack.

"Maybe it's full of money," Jacob said wishfully.

"Maybe, it's full of a bunch of clothes," Landon replied as he pulled out one piece of clothing after another.

Mason picked up the other backpack and rummaged through the contents. "Same here. Only this looks like something a woman would wear," he said, and showed his brothers a pair of feminine briefs.

"Looks like we're looking for a man and a woman then."

Mason dropped the pack and started studying the ground around them. "No, there are more. I'm seeing the same bootprints that I saw back at the field. There's a dog and a…"

"Yeah, there's a dog, and what else?" Landon asked impatiently.

"Come see for yourself."

Landon and Jacob came over and looked down at the ground where Mason was staring.

"Jesus, that looks like a bigfoot track," Jacob said.

"Sure does," Landon had to agree.

"Maybe they were hunting this thing and it got the better of them," Jacob surmised.

"Looks like two of them went off that way through those shrubs," Mason said, and pointed. He glanced down and continued to read the ground. "There's also one set of bootprints, and the dog's, heading up the trail."

"Here's what we'll do. Mason, you follow those tracks in the brush, and Jacob, you and I will continue up the trail."

"What if I find someone?" Mason asked.

"Kill them," Landon replied casually. "We only have couple hours of daylight left so you better start tracking."

"You sure you don't want me to go with you, Mason?" Jacob asked.

"No, you go ahead with Landon. I'll catch you all later."

With that said, the two brothers headed up the trail while the other one set out through the brush.

36

After Ethan had tended to the gash across his chest—which after swabbing off the blood he realized his wound really could use some stitching and would no doubt leave a ghastly scar—he'd made himself comfortable in a small nook in the rock, and before he knew it, he and Blu had fallen fast asleep.

When he finally opened his eyes, he had no idea how long he had been asleep. He looked up and gauged where the sun was positioned in the sky and figured it for late afternoon. His body felt bruised and his muscles ached from tangling with the bigfoot.

He'd been foolish thinking that he would be an equal match up against such a strong creature. Next time, he would have to play it safe, and kill the damn thing from a safe distance with his rifle. There was no point in further endangering their lives when the whole reason for even being up on this godforsaken mountain was to find Clay and Mia's son.

Ethan heard a sound coming up the trail.

"Hear that, boy? They're finally here," Ethan said to Blu, glad that the others were arriving.

But then, as he started to get to his feet, he saw that it wasn't Clay or Mia, or even Alden for that matter.

It was Micah, hobbling up the trail on his peg leg with the help of a y-shaped crutch tucked under his armpit. His face and beard were smudged with soot and his clothes were black from smoke. He was packing his Schofield revolver on his hip and had the Henry rifle strapped to his back.

"What in God's name are you doing here?" Ethan asked bewildered.

"Some yokels burned me out," Micah replied sourly.

"What in the world for?"

"Hell, I don't know. They shot up my place, then tossed in a firebomb."

"Any idea who they were?"

"Nope. But I did wing one of the bastards."

"How'd you get away?" Ethan asked.

"Went out through the mine."

"How many were they?"

"I'm pretty sure there were three. One of them called out the name Mason."

"Mason."

"That's right."

"If there were three of them that would probably mean that they were the Payne brothers. That would be Mason, Landon, and Jacob. There were four, but the youngest one's dead. We found his body down the mountain. Right where these boys have their pot field."

"So how did he die?" Micah asked.

"Don't rightly know for sure, but we think it was one of the bigfoot we've been after."

"You don't think those Payne boys think you had anything to do with it?"

"I don't see why."

"Well, I'm thinking they do. You don't go shooting someone's place up then burn it down for nothing."

"They're not exactly a friendly bunch," Ethan said.

"I don't think we should be wasting any more time just standing around," Micah said. "We need to go."

"Can't, I'm waiting for Clay, Mia, and Alden."

"Well, we can't go back there. Not with those boys hunting you. I know a place we can hold up. Not far," Micah said, leaning on his crutch but antsy to get going.

"All right. But then I'm going to have to come back."

"Hopefully, they don't meet up with those scoundrels. I'd hate if one of them was to shoot Alden."

"How far is it?" Ethan asked, grabbing his gear while Blu waited at his side.

"About a mile. It's this way," Micah said, diverting from the trail but still heading up the mountain.

37

Mason was probably the best one-eyed tracker in the entire state. But then there wasn't a contest for such an event, so there was no way of proving it. Just something that Landon always liked to say, boasting about one of his younger brothers. Even though Landon was always stern-like and had a mean streak, Mason knew that his brother loved him. Perhaps even more than Jacob and poor James on account of what their father had done.

It was back when Mason was only twelve. His father had always been a cruel son-of-a-bitch, taking out his frustration on the boys after their mother finally got sick of all the drinking and the constant beatings and packed up her things and caught the next available bus out of town.

The old man always like whaling on Mason and Jacob because he could never tell the two apart. Just looking at the twins infuriated him as he swore he was always seeing double, even when he wasn't drunk.

So one night, consumed with booze and the demon, their father came into their room, and said he was sick and tired of not knowing who was which, and with the end of a broken whiskey bottle, he plunged the tip into Mason's face.

Mason never forgot that pain, waking up, and only being able to see out of one eye. But as much as it hurt, Mason never once screamed or cried.

Payne brothers were too tough for that.

And then the torment ended after Landon threatened to kill the old man unless he left.

Mason shrugged it off and went back to what he did best: tracking. He'd scoured the area and came up with what he thought had transpired to create such footprints. The smaller impressions were of the woman. Judging by the way she had come, she must have left the group on her own, perhaps to take a squat.

Then the man had followed but on a different path.

Mason walked through a berry patch and stopped. The ground was churned up in one spot as if an animal had been rolling around in the dirt. He saw a splattering here and there of purplish pools, but after dipping his finger, discovered that it was berry juice and not blood as he first suspected.

He followed the prints through a thicket of brush to the edge of a ravine. He looked down at the steep drop off, which if he was right, meant that the man and woman had fallen down there, but he didn't see anyone.

If he shimmied down, there was a good chance that he wouldn't be able to climb back up. He looked to his left and saw that the gorge came to a dead end as if there had been an avalanche long ago that had blocked it off. They could have only gone one way.

He could walk along the top of the ridge, but as the canyon took a bend farther up, he decided that it would be better to just cut across and shorten the distance and possibly catch up to them at the other side of the gorge.

**

Mason strode through the woods figuring that he if he kept it up, he would soon be at the rim of the ridge, and if he were lucky, would spot the couple down below.

In his heart, he wanted them to be James' killers, because what was the point of shooting them, if they weren't? Even though he had done some killing, he didn't really enjoy seeing others die.

But then he never wanted to disappoint Landon, no matter what his brother told him to do. If he wanted these two killed, well, that was what he was going to do.

With that in mind, he quickened his pace.

His foot came down on nothing, not dirt, not ground, nothing.

Mason fell straight down into a tubular shaft.

And kept falling.

38

The setting sun dipped behind the tall trees on the ridge, casting eerie shadows down into the gorge.

"It's getting cold," Mia said, wrapping her arms around her chest to keep warm.

"We need to find somewhere to hold up for the night," Clay said.

They were approaching a large boulder and had lost sight of Alden who was a fair distance in front of them.

"I wish he'd slow down," Mia said.

"Yeah, we surely don't want to lose him. It'll be dark soon. We better find him," Clay said, walking a little faster.

Mia picked up her stride as well to keep up.

They were just rounding the boulder when they saw Alden standing on a ledge atop a sloping embankment twenty feet up from the basin. The bigfoot was pacing and looked impatient, like he had been waiting there for days when in reality it couldn't have been more that a couple of minutes.

"We're coming," Mia said, reading his body language.

It was a fairly easy climb.

Clay and Mia were quite surprised when they reached the ledge where Alden was standing and saw the five cave entrances. Only the one in the middle was high enough for them to enter walking upright as the other four caves were only three or four feet in diameter.

"What do you make of that?" Mia asked.

"Look like burrows," Clay said. He approached one of the smaller holes, got down on his hands and knees, and peered inside. "It seems to go back a ways."

Alden had already ventured into the largest cave.

"Maybe we can spend the night in there," Mia said.

Clay got to his feet and followed Mia.

Upon entering the cave, they saw that there was a long tunnel that stretched for a considerable distance. Normally, it should have been pitch black at the far side of the passage, but for some reason, there was light filtering down from the ceiling in various spots.

As they walked in, Clay stopped at the first light source and looked up. He had to crane his neck all the way back so that he could look straight up the narrow shaft that went all the way up to the surface—more than fifty feet up—where he could just make out a pinprick of purple sky.

"What do you think caused that?" Clay said after Mia had taken a look up the shaft.

"Some natural erosion, I suppose."

They saw that Alden was getting ahead of them.

"There he goes again," Mia said.

"Alden!" Clay shouted. "Hold up!"

Clay and Mia hurried after the bigfoot, and had almost caught up to him, when suddenly, there was a loud crash up ahead.

"What the hell was that?" Clay said.

Clay pointed the muzzle of his rifle at the ground, ready to fire if need be.

Alden was standing to one side, staring down at a large black mass in the middle of the passageway.

"What is it? A bear?" Mia asked, as she got closer.

"No, it's a man," Clay said. The unconscious man had a grisly black beard and an eye-patch. He wore a thick black coat, black jeans, and dark-colored boots.

"He kind of looks like a cross between a pirate and a mountain man," Mia quipped.

Clay gazed up the shaft that the man had just fallen down. "Well, now we know what a swallow hole is."

Alden began to growl when he saw the man's hand move.

"Clay, he's waking up. His guns," Mia warned.

Clay reached down and grabbed the machinegun. He also took away the man's handgun and hunting knife.

"Wha…just…happened…?" the man said, pushing himself up into a sitting position. As soon as he saw Clay and Mia, he immediately reached for his weapons. "Hey, what the hell!"

Clay pointed his rifle at the man's chest. "Just relax, and stay right where you are."

When the man turned, he saw Alden, and for a moment, Clay thought the man might scream out with alarm, even though that seemed unlikely, as the man and Alden were pretty close to the same size.

"Give me my gun so I can shoot this thing," the man snarled.

"You'll do not such thing," Mia said. "Alden's our friend."

"Friend? Are you two out of your mind? This monster killed my brother."

"Where was this?" Clay asked.

"Down the mountain."

"Was it by a pot field?"

"Yeah, how the hell did you know that?"

"We went through there looking for a band of bigfoot," Clay said.

"They stole our baby," Mia added.

"And this bigfoot's not one of them?" the man said, still glaring at Alden.

"No. Like I said, he's our friend, and his helping us find our boy."

"So, what, your boy was kidnapped?"

"That's right. They broke into our cabin a few nights ago and took him. I have no idea why."

"I might. While we were burying James, he's the one that was killed, we found a dead bigfoot baby in the field."

"Was it gray?"

"Yep. We reckon James must have shot it."

"Oh my God," Mia said and clamped her hand over her mouth.

"Who are you?" Clay asked.

"Mason Payne. My brothers and I have been dogging your trail."

"Why?"

"Landon thinks you killed our brother, James."

"Landon's your other brother."

"Yeah, there's him and Jacob."

"But we're telling you that it wasn't us," Clay said.

"Then, I guess I'm inclined to believe you. Didn't feel much like killing you anyway."

"Well, that's a relief," Mia said sarcastically.

"So, can I have my guns back?"

"Can we trust you?"

"You mean, am I a man of my word? I guess you'll just have to find out and see."

Clay and Mia looked at each other thinking they would be able to make a collaborative decision, but they were stymied. Either Mason was going to join them, or he was going to turn on them. There was no way of really knowing.

"Here," Clay said, and placed Mason's guns and knife on the ground within reach.

"So, what is this place?" Mason asked as he got to his feet.

"We're not really sure. Leads somewhere into the mountain," Clay said.

Mia looked up and noticed that the passageway was beginning to get dark as it was close to sundown.

Mason pulled out a flashlight out of his rucksack and led the way.

39

They hadn't traveled more than a quarter of a mile through the tunnel when they came across a side passage, which was only waist high. Mason ducked down and shined the flashlight down the narrow corridor.

"It looks like it connects to another tunnel."

"Probably one of those smaller caves we saw," Clay said.

"Let's keep going," Mia said.

Mason panned the flashlight in front of him and started following the beam.

While they walked, Mason noted two more side routes but didn't stop.

"There must be tunnels all through this mountain," Clay said.

"There's a large cavern up ahead," Manson said.

The antechamber was dome-shaped and enormous, the highest point on the concaved ceiling well over thirty feet up.

Thousands of bleached-white bones—from apparent years of accumulation—were scattered in large six-foot tall heaps.

"What is this place?" Mia said.

"Some animal's lair," Mason replied.

Clay stepped over to a mound of bones littered with shredded animal hides. "What do you think, Mason? You're the hunter."

Mason walked over and inspected the bones. "Looks like small animals mostly, rabbits and rodents, a lot of birds."

Alden was pacing again, definitely agitated being surrounded by so much death.

"You better see this," Mia said, staring down at a mound of more skeletal remains.

Clay and Mason came over and looked at the pile made up of larger-sized bones.

Mason leaned down and picked up a skull.

It looked almost human but with a flat, broader forehead and a low-hanging jawbone and was twice the size of any person.

"Is that what I think it is?" Clay asked.

"Yeah, it's a bigfoot skull," Mason confirmed.

Alden bellowed as though he were suddenly being subjected to a torturous pain.

Mia could see that Alden was clearly upset. "Alden, it's all right."

Clay glanced around at the other stacks of bones. "My God, there're more of them. What could it possibly be?"

"Whatever it is, it's big enough to hunt bigfoot," Mason said.

"I don't have a good feeling about this place," Mia said. "We really need to leave."

"I agree, but there's really no point going back the way we came," Clay said.

"Maybe we don't have to." Mia pointed to a section of wall where actual steps had been chiseled out of the porous rock, leading up to what appeared a hole in the ceiling.

"Let's get out of here," Manson said with a sense of urgency.

40

By the time Clay scaled up, and joined the others standing amongst the trees, it was pitch-dark with only a sliver of moonlight illuminating the forest.

"Do you think you'll be able to pick up their tracks?" Clay asked.

"Not until morning," Mason replied.

"I think we should get as far away from here as we can before we decide to camp anywhere," Mia said.

"I agree," Mason said.

Alden turned and headed for a break in the brush.

"Does he know where he's going?" Mason asked.

"Well, he's gotten us this far," Mia said.

"Let's go before we lose him in the dark," Clay said.

They made their way through the forest, partly guided by Mason's flashlight, but mostly by Alden's keen nose.

Satisfied that they had distanced themselves far enough away from the bizarre boneyard back in the cavern, Mason soon spotted a recessed area between some boulders that was protected on three sides and would be the perfect place to spend the rest of the night.

Mason elected to stand first watch.

Even though it was chilly, they decided against having a campfire, as they didn't want to give their position away.

Clay and Mia cuddled up to stay warm while Alden sat on his side with his head lulled on his chest, fast asleep. Soon, he began to snore, loudly.

"That is so annoying," Clay said. He leaned over and elbowed Alden in the ribs, but the bigfoot continued to snuffle and snort.

Clay groaned and closed his eyes.

41

Ethan was amazed by the old-timer's endurance, as not once, did Micah want to stop and rest, hobbling on his peg leg with only the help of his crutch.

"So where are we going?" Ethan asked as he tried not to stumble over Blu in the dark as the coonhound had a bad habit of cutting in front of him, especially when the path they were following veered from a straight line.

"The cabin where I grew up," Micah replied over his shoulder.

"Does anyone live there anymore?"

"I would hardly think so. My folks have been dead for many years."

They were just coming up on a rise when Ethan saw the backwoods lodge tucked back in the trees under the moonlight. The place didn't appear to be occupied, as there were no lights shining from the windows.

Micah limped up onto the porch and pushed open the front door. Before he could set foot inside, a bird or a bat, screeched as it flew out into the night.

"Damn near scared me half to death," Micah said, but didn't hesitate to go inside.

Ethan shooed Blu through the front door and walked in after.

Micah fumbled around in the dark for a moment before striking a match and lighting the wick on a lantern. Soon, the interior of the cabin came into view as the bulb brightened.

"It ain't much, but it's a roof over our heads," Micah boasted.

Ethan looked up and saw that some of the rafters and shake had come down as he could see a patch of moonlit sky through the gap in the roof. He didn't say anything, as he didn't want to sound ungrateful.

The cabin looked similar to Micah's place, basic and slightly bigger with one bunk, a long table and two bench seats, and a door that led into another room. Some uncovered wooden crates were against one wall.

Ethan walked over and looked inside one of the boxes and saw the tops of evenly spaced Mason jars. He reached down, picked up a jar, and unscrewed the lid. He took a big whiff.

"Try it," Micah said.

Ethan took a gulp and almost coughed as the fiery liquid burned down his gullet.

"That's my folks' special blend. Peels paint better than turpentine."

"I bet it does."

"Take another swig and pass it over."

Ethan did just that. This time, the pure alcohol wasn't as harsh as his throat was already numb from the first drink. It reminded him of the last time he tried siphoning gasoline out of his truck and ended up swallowing a mouthful of petrol when he sucked too hard on the plastic tube.

"I haven't been up here in over thirty years," Micah said, taking another swig and gazing about the dilapidated cabin. "There's a still nearby, in a cavern where my daddy used to make shine. I doubt if there's much of it left. We can go take a look tomorrow."

"You can. I have to go back for the others."

"There's a tunnel that goes back in there, comes out in a small valley. I can show you a shortcut."

"All right," Ethan agreed.

"Then it's settled." Micah passed Ethan the jar.

Even though the ruined cabin didn't keep out the elements and the temperature had dropped outside, it was doubtful if either man was going to feel the cold.

42

Unable to pick up the tracks in the dark, and wandering aimlessly, Landon and Jacob finally gave up for the night as they were exhausted. They set up camp on a hummock surrounded by rocks and ferns. Jacob collected deadwood and built a small campfire while Landon divvied out small portions of food.

After they had eaten their meager meals, Landon said he would stand the second watch and found a comfortable bed of pine needles to sleep on while Jacob stayed up and kept guard for the first shift.

But after an hour, Jacob began to wane and started to nod off—and soon drifted off to sleep, with his shotgun lying across his lap.

Jacob suddenly awoke when he felt a sharp jab in his leg.

"Shit," he cursed under his breath when he realized that he had fallen asleep when Landon trusted him to be on watch.

He gazed up and saw three figures standing over him in the silver moonlight.

They couldn't have been more than three feet tall. It was difficult to determine their age in the dim lighting, but Jacob was certain they weren't children. They wore animal skins and were barefoot.

Their large, hairless craniums were disproportionate to their small bodies.

The one to his right was wearing a hide open in the front, its prominent clavicles and ribcage visible under its thin parchment skin that looked as though it had been tanned and stretched over its skeletal frame.

He couldn't see their eyes clearly as they were recessed in deep-set sockets. None of them possessed noses, just air holes for nasal passages.

They were armed with four-foot long pointy-tipped lances, and knife-like spearheads made of flint.

The three humanoids—which strongly resembled pigmy ghouls—snarled, exposing squared incisors caked with black tartar and gunk.

Jacob's hand slowly slid along the stock of the shotgun, his finger itching for the trigger.

The creatures lunged in unison, like warriors ordered by a silent command, and speared Jacob. He tried moving his right leg, but his calf was impaled to the ground. The one that had stabbed him in the chest was already withdrawing its lance and preparing to run him through again. The third spear that had been thrust in his side was giving him serious pain, as it had to have punctured a vital organ.

"Landon!" Jacob screamed. He turned his head and saw a dozen silhouettes converging on the campsite. Some of them were carrying large rocks while the others were armed with cudgels and spears.

Jacob lifted his shotgun and fired into the nearest creature. The heavy-load buckshot blasted apart its upper body into tiny splintering pieces like it was made of thin balsa wood. He slid back the pump, shoved another cartridge in the chamber, and disintegrated another attacker but not before it thrust its spear into Jacob's windpipe.

Landon was already on his feet, aiming the Marlin lever-action and firing at the creatures until the 4-round clip went dry.

But they kept coming.

He flipped the rifle around, and used it like a baseball bat; smashing one in the face, and cracking another across the skull, sending them both to the ground.

He counted maybe seven of them, forming a circle around him.

Landon drew his high-caliber revolver and started to pivot slowly, picking off one creature at a time as if he were performing a bizarre target practice.

Two of them came up from behind and thrust their spears into Landon's back. He spun around, pulling one spear out of his flesh, the other breaking off and still stuck in the wound. He fired off two shots, killing each of his attackers.

A spear flew over the campfire and lodged in Landon's shoulder. He grabbed the shaft and yanked it out. Another spear struck his thigh. He leaned down and managed to pull that one out. Rocks began to hail in his direction.

He fell to one knee and grabbed a fistful of cartridges out of his coat pocket. He pushed the extractor lever and rolled out the cylinder. He dumped out the spent shells onto the ground, and started pressing fresh bullets into the cylinder.

Another humanoid came at him.

With only two bullets in, Landon flipped the cylinder closed, and fired both shots into the pigmy ghoul's chest. He staggered to his feet, stumbled over and braced against a tree trunk to reload his gun.

He glanced up, expecting at any second to be stabbed or pummeled with a rock then realized that he was no longer of prime interest as there was more of them milled around Jacob's body.

Landon watched in horror as they gathered up his brother and carted him away.

***

It took ten of them to carry the big man through the forest. Once they arrived at the gaping hole in the ground, they commenced stripping the clothing from the body, slashing through the garments and flesh with their sharp weapons and tearing away the shreds with their vicious hands.

Picking up their prey, they positioned the head over the hole then shoved the naked body down into the boneyard pit thirty feet below where it landed with a loud, sickening, bone-splintering crunch.

One by one, the pygmy ghouls descended the stone steps into their lair where a hundred or more creatures were already waiting to start their nighttime feast.

43

The morning sun glared down through the opening in the rotted roof and shined down into Micah's face, waking him up. He sat up and slid his good leg over the side of the bunk and placed his barefoot on the floorboard. Wearing only a ratty pair of shorts, he reached over and inserted his stump into the peg leg and fastened the strap around his waist.

He stood up and lightly tapped the bottom of the artificial limb to ensure that his stump had a comfortable fit.

The sound woke up Ethan, who was lying on the stiff floor. He started to get up but immediately decided against any sudden moves and lay back down. "I swear, my head's about to come off."

"It'll pass," Micah said. "You got any food?"

"You might find something in my bag," Ethan said as he slowly sat up then gingerly got to his feet. That's when he realized that he must have passed out the night before because he was still in his clothes.

Micah rummaged through Ethan's backpack and came up with a couple of biscuits wrapped in butcher paper. "Here, you go," he said, handing a roll to Ethan. "This should soak up some of that booze."

"Much obliged," Ethan said, thanking Micah for a biscuit that was rightfully his.

After they had forced down the dry, stale dinner rolls and drank some water from Ethan's canteen, Micah finished getting dressed and put on his boot. They collected their rifles and side arms and went outside.

Micah led the way around the side of the cabin to a pathway that stretched into the trees. They hadn't gone far when they reached a large entrance to a cave. The opening was around twenty feet wide and fifteen feet high.

As Micah and Ethan walked in, they could hear the dripping and feel the chill associated with a wet cave. Turquoise phosphorus lichen glistened on the limestone interior walls.

Fifty feet in, they came upon a subterranean aquifer and an abandoned bootleg distillery operation set up on a granite bank. Goose-necked and long lengths of copper piping—longed turned green from age—were still connected to a five rusted derelict boilers.

There were 50-gallon barrels lined up against a curved wall, others stacked on top of each other, maybe a hundred casks altogether.

Metal flecks drifted in the underground pool beneath the scummy, viscous surface. A heavy cloying stink permeated the dank air—a mix of decay, rust, and high-octane alcohol.

"Looks like your folks ran a pretty big operation here," Ethan said.

"No, they only had one still," Micah said. "This belonged to someone else."

"You don't think *they* were the owners?" Ethan pointed over to the corpses lying next to one of the boilers.

There were four bodies. They were mere skeletons under the rotted clothes and appeared to have been there for decades.

"They must have had a grievance," Micah said.

"Looks like there were no winners." Ethan wandered over to one of the copper boilers, the base sitting on top of a slate kiln. He gazed at the copper piping connected to the other boilers, trying to make sense of the process. "So how does this work?"

"It's simple enough. Grind up some cornmeal and boil it up. Let it cool then throw in some sugar, add the yeast. Then let it sit for a few days to ferment into sour mash. Then you cook it up until it steams through those coils," Micah said, pointing at the copper tubing attached to the tops of the boilers. "It travels down those pipes and out comes your liquid moonshine."

"How dangerous was it, making moonshine?" Ethan asked.

"You mean, could you blow yourself up? You bet."

44

Mason waded through the ground fog looking for any signs of tracks, but it was useless as most of the time he couldn't even see his boots.

"Anything?" Clay asked.

"I can't see a damn thing."

Mia looked around at the morning mist that covered the forest floor, obscuring the trees off in the distance.

Alden ambled up to the front of the line and went ahead of Mason. The bigfoot didn't look back, just kept shambling into the dense, waist-high mist.

"Looks like Alden's picked up a scent," Clay said.

"Or he's just taking a walk in the woods," Mason said.

"Either way, we better not lose him." Mia hurried after Alden.

"Yeah, she's right. Be easy in this pea soup."

Mason and Clay jogged after Mia until they caught up to Alden—and luckily, they had picked up the pace—as now the bigfoot was lengthening his stride and gliding through the ground fog with a purpose.

***

They were lying on the ground, gazing down a declivity that stretched down into a vale of brushwood where a clan of gray-haired bigfoot were foraging berries and fruit blossoms.

"I count twenty," Clay said.

"Twenty-one," Mason corrected. "There's another one by that tree stump."

"You're right. I see it now."

Alden lay anxiously next to Mia.

"Are they your family?" Mia asked the bigfoot, using their hand language.

Alden replied that he was unsure.

"What did he say?" Clay asked Mia.

"He doesn't know."

"Hey, look over there," Mason said, pointing a fair distance away where three other bigfoot were scrunched behind a hedge.

"It's the black and brown," Clay said. "The ones we've been after."

"There's the female," Mia said, spotting the smaller, gray-furred bigfoot sitting on the ground with a tiny blond head tucked in the crook of her massive arm.

"I see Casey."

"We need to go down there and get him," Clay said.

"But how? We charge down there, the female will run off, and the others will attack us. Not to mention that group over there," Mia said, tilting her head in the direction of the gray tribe.

"Why do you think those three are keeping to themselves?" Clay asked.

"Maybe they don't get along with the others," Mason replied.

"You don't think the female is an outcast, and she joined up with those other two?"

"Could be they're all outcasts which might explain why they came down off the mountain," Mia said.

"Well, if we're going to get your boy, we're going to need a plan," Mason said.

Mia and Clay nodded in agreement.

The three had been so engrossed talking and spying on the bigfoot they never realized Alden had slipped away until they looked over and saw that he was gone.

45

The first thing Ethan and Micah noticed when they returned to the cabin was the trail of blood on the dirt leading up the porch and under the closed door.

"Looks like we might have company," Micah said, cocking his Schofield.

Ethan drew his forty-five. He approached the door and nudged it open with his boot. As soon as Blu peered through the doorway, his hackles shot up.

They stepped inside and found a man slumped on the bunk with his back up against the wall. His jacket and pants were covered in blood. A rifle was lying on the mattress next to his right hand.

"Landon?" Ethan said, recognizing one of the Payne brothers.

"Ethan, what the hell you doing here?"

"That's a question for you," Micah said, pointing his revolver at the man bleeding all over his bed.

"We've been hunting whoever killed my brother."

"That would be James, I gather," Ethan said.

"Yeah, how'd you know?"

"We were passing by your field when we found him. We thought it only fitting to wrap him up and put him in the cave."

"You did that?"

"That's right. We've been after some bigfoot that stole my nephew's baby boy."

"Strange, we found a dead baby bigfoot out in the field," Landon said.

"Well, don't that beat all," Micah said. "Swapped one for the other."

"So what happened to you?" Ethan asked.

"Jacob and I got ambushed by these…things. Hell, I don't know what they were. Looked like little demons. Weren't more than three feet tall. They killed Jacob and hauled away his body. They got me pretty good."

"Sounds like you had a run-in with the little people," Micah said.

"Whoa," Ethan said. "I thought you said that was only a legend."

"Did I? Well, I guess I was mistaken. They're real, all right. Why do you think I moved away from this part of the mountain?"

"So it was only the two of you?" Ethan asked Landon.

"No. We got split up. I have no idea where Mason is."

"Mason! I heard someone yell out that name before some yahoos started shooting up my place then burned me out. That was you?" Micah aimed his gun at Landon, just as the other man reached for his rifle.

"Hey, hey," Ethan shouted, standing in the middle of the two quarreling men. "Shooting each other isn't going to do us any good. Just put them down."

Blu joined in and snarled, sensing the men's anger.

The men kept eyeballing each other, but then they finally laid down their weapons.

"Good." Ethan stepped back and Blu quieted down. He looked at Landon. "So, when was the last time you saw your brother?"

"When we came across a couple of backpacks and I sent him off to track down the owners."

"That would have been my nephew and his wife. What was he going to do when he found them?"

Landon didn't say anything.

"Well?"

"I told him to kill them."

46

Even though they were concerned not knowing why Alden had snuck off and were worried for his safety, it didn't deter them from the task at hand. After some brief discussion, they finally came up with a course of action.

It was a simple enough plan.

Mason would create a diversion to draw the two male bigfoot away from the female, while Clay and Mia went in and rescued their son.

They crept along the top of the knoll until they found underbrush tall enough that they could venture down behind and not be detected.

When they finally made it to the hollow without arousing suspicion, they ducked behind a stand of shrubs for cover. From their vantage point, they could see the black and brown bigfoot twenty feet away by themselves, squatting on the ground and grabbing handfuls of elderberries off a plant and stuffing the fruit into their greedy mouths.

The female was sitting on the ground with her back against a tree. Her chin was slumped on her chest, Casey lying on her lap, both sound asleep taking a nap.

"This is our chance," Clay whispered.

Mason peered through the branches and stole a peek at the two males. "Okay, give me a slow count to thirty then make your move."

"Be careful," Mia said.

Mason was taken aback. "I don't think anyone's ever said that to me before." He gave her smile—a yellow crescent in his fuzzy beard.

The big man crept away and edged along the underbrush until he reached an area of deadfall and hid behind a large log. He wet his finger, put it up to test the air, and felt a slight breeze blowing in his face, which meant that he was downwind of the two bigfoot and they probably hadn't picked up his scent though he could surely smell their stench.

Mason looked down at the ground and saw a large pinecone. He picked it up and threw it as far as he could deeper into the woods. The strobile struck a tree trunk with a loud *crack* and bounced off onto the dirt.

The black bigfoot was the first to hear the sound and looked in the general direction where Mason had thrown the pinecone. Mason waited for it to wander over to investigate the sound, but the creature didn't move. Time was running out. He picked up another pinecone. He needed to draw their attention to him.

So he stood up and made himself visible to the two creatures.

"Hey!" Then Mason threw the pinecone, striking the brown bigfoot in the face.

The creature snarled, jumped to its feet, and immediately charged.

Mason backed away and began running, baiting the angry animal as it got tangled in the brush. The plan was working—maybe too well—because the black bigfoot was also in pursuit, and with its great bulk, was steamrolling through the barrier of shrubs like the vegetation wasn't even there.

He ran as fast as he could, knowing at any time that he could spin around and kill them with his AR-15, but that meant alarming the bigfoot clan not too far away, and spooking the female before Clay and Mia could get a chance to grab Casey.

Mason had no choice but to run for his life.

***

"Come on," Clay whispered to Mia. They squeezed between the bushes and tread softly toward the slumbering bigfoot. Each step was excruciatingly slow as there were broken branches and twigs everywhere on the ground. One false move was all it would take and their hopes of saving their little boy would be gone.

Clay had his rifle ready in case the bigfoot should wake suddenly and lash out at them. Mia was right by his side as they moved in, each one careful not to…

Snap.

Mia looked down at her boot in disbelief and saw the end of a twig sticking out from under her rubber sole.

The female bolted awake. She took in the two figures standing in front of her and in a split second was on her feet, crashing into the brush with Casey tucked under her arm, and was gone before Clay and Mia even knew what was happening.

47

Once Mason had lured the two bigfoot far enough away, giving Clay and Mia hopefully the time they needed to retrieve their son, he stopped and turned around to stand his ground. He raised the muzzle of the AR-15 to take aim on the first bigfoot to appear in his gun sight.

The black bigfoot stormed out of the trees.

Mason set his finger in the trigger guard, waited for the precise moment, and pulled the trigger.

The machinegun only clicked.

It was jammed.

Before Mason could go for his sidearm, the black bigfoot was already smashing into his body, knocking him to the ground. A mallet fist came down and slammed Mason's skull. The creature reared back for another assault. But before the wrecking ball could rain down again, Mason drew his Ruger nine-millimeter.

He rolled his head and shoulder, jammed the gun muzzle in the black bigfoot's gut, and pulled the trigger. The gunshot was muffled in the animal's thick fur.

The bigfoot roared as it rose, clamping its hand over the gunshot wound.

Mason could see a funnel of blood oozing out. There was also dried blood across its chest from a previous injury, and when it pulled its bloody hand away from its stomach, Mason could see a gaping hole clear through its palm.

No longer wanting to be in the fight, the black bigfoot held its belly wound and staggered into the trees.

Mason was too busy watching the gunshot bigfoot run off that he forgot about the other one. When he turned, he was already too late. The brown bigfoot stomped down on his gun hand, snapping his trigger finger in the guard, and breaking his thumb.

"Jesus!" Mason yelped.

The bigfoot came down again, this time driving the heel of its enormous foot down onto Mason's ribcage. The air was instantly punched out of his lungs. A sharp pain cut into his side most likely the result of a cracked rib. He coughed and gasped and tried to sit up, but he was too spent to move. He looked over at his gun in the dirt, but his hand was useless to pick it up.

He was a goner, and he knew it. Even if he was to pull out his knife, he didn't have the strength to protect himself.

All he could do was lie there, and wait. Wait for…

A gray blur came out of nowhere and rammed into the brown bigfoot.

Mason turned his head.

And was never so happy to see Alden.

Mason had never witnessed such a savage brawl. Both creatures were punching, tearing at each other's fur, and fiercely biting one another. They were growling, spittle and blood flying out of their mouths.

Alden kicked at the other bigfoot. When the creature fell back on the ground, Alden picked up a large rock with both hands, and with a mighty downswing, crushed his opponent's skull in. The brown bigfoot's body and legs shuddered for a moment, and then it was dead.

Still lying on his back, Mason stared through the treetops and gazed up at the sky, thinking he was never more thankful to be alive.

48

Clay and Mia dashed after the female, surprised at how fast the large creature could run. They had caught fleeting glimpses of the fleeing bigfoot as she charged through the thorny briars, leaving swaths of her fur behind. Instead of sprinting on her hind legs, she was loping on her left front hand and hind legs, carrying Casey close to her body like a primate protecting her young, stampeding through a jungle.

"I thought they would be slow," Clay called over his shoulder as he darted between the trees, doing his best to keep up the chase.

"She must be frightened out of her mind," Mia shouted. Even though she was a small-framed woman, she had a long stride and was right on Clay's heels.

Clay was just rounding a high scrub when he saw the bigfoot scamper up to a cave entrance set in the granite face of the hillside and rush inside. He slowed down his pace to a walk.

"What's wrong? Why are you stopping?" Mia asked, almost running into her husband as she, too, stumbled to a halt.

"She went in there," Clay said, pointing to the opening.

They approached the mouth of the gloomy cave, not knowing if the bigfoot was laying a trap, waiting to jump out at them the second they stepped inside.

"I can't see where they went," Clay said, staring into the caliginous tunnel.

He went in first. Mia stayed close. Even though the passage ahead was tenebrous, there were fissures of natural daylight shinning down from the ceiling. Clay and Mia looked up as they walked and could see tiny patches of blue sky through the narrow clefts in the rock stretching all the way up to the surface. The stone floor and walls were damp and slick from condensation and water seepage.

Clay looked down at the ground and saw large wet footprints. "We're in luck."

"Come on, she couldn't have gotten far," Mia said.

They wanted to run, but the slick rock was too slippery, so they kept it to a fast walk, grabbing at the walls whenever they thought they were going to slide and fall.

Clay and Mia crossed over some dry ground, and the footprints soon faded away just as they reached a junction of four dark passages.

"Now what do we do?" Mia said painfully.

49

Mason returned to where he had left Clay and Mia and quickly picked up their tracks. He could tell by their deep imprints that there had been a pursuit.

His hand hurt like hell from resetting his thumb and forefinger, which were purple and swollen. Even though he wasn't much of a shot with his left hand, he still carried the gun with him.

Alden, too, was following their trail with his nose.

After covering a fair amount of ground, they stopped at a hedgerow of shrubs.

Mason could see the dark entrance to a cave.

He was about to step out of the bushes when Alden grunted a warning. Mason didn't know if he should heed the admonisher hunkered down by his side but figured he better, trusting Alden's acute instincts.

That's when he saw the fierce-looking ghoul step out from the trees. He had never seen such a creature. Even though it resembled a short person, it was definitely not human. It looked like a walking skeleton with paper-thin skin.

The barefoot ghoul stood, wielding a spear. It wore a white animal hide across its shoulders, opened in the front, a mummified snow fox's snout face as a headdress.

Mason had never seen anything more ugly.

It was straight out of a nightmare.

The miniature warrior tramped over to the cave entrance and peered into the murkiness. It knelt on one bony knee, swiped the ground with its thin-fingered hand, and licked its palm with a black, serpentine tongue.

The ghoul stood, faced the trees, and trilled like a raccoon.

Mason watched in horror, as one by one, more similar-looking creatures appeared, all dressed in animal skins and carrying lances.

They gradually mustered into small groups.

Mason counted more than a hundred.

The abomination that had summoned the others, which Mason assumed was their leader, pointed his spear at the cave entrance, signaling the horde to enter.

Mason stayed behind his concealment until the last ghoul had gone inside.

"It's a damn hunting party," he said and turned his head.

Alden was no longer by his side.

He had skulked off while Mason had been enthralled watching the strange creatures assembling.

"Not again." This time, he was mad. "Where the hell did you go? Don't tell me you're scared?" he cursed, accusing the bigfoot of being petrified and slinking away.

"Oh, what the hell." Mason pushed through the shrubs, and with his pistol in hand, strode toward the cave.

50

"Maybe we should split up. That would give us a fifty-fifty chance," Mia said, trying to rationalize their options as she stared at the four passageways.

"And if we choose the wrong ones? We'd most likely get lost and never find each other. No, we have to stay together. Just pick one."

Still indecisive, Mia stepped from one passage entrance to the other, and then, suddenly stopped at the third one. "She went through here. I can smell her."

Clay rushed over and sniffed the air. "You're right. Let's go."

"Wait a sec. Do you hear that?"

Clay turned his head to listen, thinking that Mia had heard something up ahead.

"No," Mia said when she realized he had misunderstood her. "Behind us. Do you hear that?"

Clay turned his head. "Yeah, I do. Sounds like an army coming."

"An army of what?"

"Bigfoot?"

"We have to hide. And quick."

They ran into the passage that they were sure the female bigfoot had taken. The corridor wound through the rock in twisty turns. They could hear footfalls approaching steadily from behind.

In a matter of seconds, the creatures would be around the bend.

Clay looked up. "We can hide up there." He pointed to a recess in the wall up near the ceiling. He put his hands together, interweaving his fingers. "Here, step up."

Mia placed her boot in his hands and let Clay boost her up. She grabbed hold and pulled herself into the niche that was situated eight feet up from the ground. Clay climbed up and crammed into the cranny next to Mia.

Clay was afraid that when the tall creatures ran by, their hidey-hole wouldn't be high enough, and the bigfoot would easily spot them as they passed by.

The couple heard bare feet slapping across the stone floor below, but they couldn't see who it was. Edging toward the lip, Clay and Mia gazed down.

A dozen short creatures with spears raced by.

"Oh my God, Clay. Are those…the little people?" Mia gasped.

"Jesus, Micah wasn't lying."

And that's when they heard the female bigfoot's terrified cry.

51

Hustling through the passageway, the female bigfoot howled when she realized that she had run into a dead end. She was standing in a small antechamber with nowhere to go. Above her head was an airshaft that went up to the surface, but it wasn't within her reach.

Her baby was agitated from all the jostling and began to wail. She was frightened, trapped. She glanced around to see if there was a possibility of scaling the walls, anything to get out of this prison, escape the danger that she had so unwontedly put the two of them in.

And then they scurried in; the ones that hunted her kind. Even though she was bigger and stronger, they greatly outnumbered her, and she was further disadvantaged having to protect her baby.

She backed against a wall so that they couldn't outflank her and placed the baby on the ground behind her foot. She rolled her shoulders and puffed out her chest and roared at the troupe forming in front of her. They stood side by side, pointing their sharp spears.

Their gaze was not so much on her as it was on her crying baby. They were a vicious lot. She had seen them attack before. The way they pleasured in killing.

Three of them came at her at once. With both hands free, she swatted a weapon out of one assailant's tiny hands. Another one lunged, and she avoided being stabbed by stepping to one side.

Giving the third aggressor the perfect opportunity to impale her in the abdomen.

She screeched, reached down, and plucked out the shaft. Then she grabbed her tormenter by the throat, slammed its skull into the rock wall, smashing it open like a gooey gourd.

Another one got too close and she hammered her fist, driving its head down through its spine.

She fought courageously, but the beset became overwhelming as more of them advanced, thrusting and jabbing, most often connecting and drawing gouts of blood every time they jerked their spear tips out of her body.

She howled, not so much because of the pain, but knowing that it was only a matter of time before she would no longer be able to shield her baby from the bloodthirsty predators.

A daring assailant ran up and drove its weapon into her chest.

The female bigfoot dropped to her knees.

She raised her arms to ward off more punishing strikes and further impalements as her baby cried at the top of his lungs.

The infant's unrest only fueled the murderous lot to quicken the job.

52

"That's Casey crying," Mia said, hearing her son further down the passage as she scooted down from their hiding place into Clay's waiting arms.

Clay and Mia took off running as now their son's capturer was bellowing in pain.

"They must be after her," Mia said.

"Sounds like they caught up," Clay responded.

When they came around a bend, they almost ran smack dab into the pack of little people converging on the fallen bigfoot.

"Get away from her," Mia yelled.

Ten ghouls turned in unison and pointed their sharp spears. Four of them even charged.

Clay raised the Winchester and shot one in the chest. The creature screeched and fell dead on the ground. He levered another round and fired, killing another one. The other two stepped back to regroup with the others.

Three ghouls came at Mia. She pulled her small handgun out of her coat pocket and began shooting, dropping two in their tracks.

The third one snarled, ready to run her through...

Clay shot Mia's attacker in the head. The creature's skull splintered apart like a porcelain teacup.

When the others ran at them, Clay levered a couple more shots as Mia emptied her .22 caliber. The remainder of the group dispersed and ran back through the cave.

Mia approached the mortally wounded bigfoot.

Down on her haunches and propped up against the wall, her riddled body was covered in bloody splotches. Close to death, she reached down and picked up Casey, who was still fussing. She cradled him in her arms and he instantly quieted down.

Looking down, Mia couldn't help but cry.

Even though this creature had abducted her son and stolen him away, Mia was grateful that Casey had been cared for. This massive beast that lay here before her had actually sacrificed her life in order to keep her son from being harmed.

Mia knelt on the ground. "I'm so sorry." She reached out and placed her hand on the bigfoot's arm. Mia gave the hand sign for 'thank you' even though she doubted if the animal would understand.

The female bigfoot nodded her head that she understood. She raised her hand to pass Casey over to his rightful mother, but the infant protested and continued to cling to the bigfoot's fur.

After a few failed attempts at exchanging the baby, Casey eventually let go, and Mia took her son into her arms.

Clay came over and put his arm around Mia's shoulder. "Finally, we have our boy back."

But the joyful moment was cut short when they realized that the female bigfoot was dead.

Mia unzipped her jacket and placed Casey inside even though he stunk. She partially zipped up the front in a makeshift papoose.

"Now we can get off this godforsaken mountain," Clay said as he reloaded his rifle and they started back through the cave.

53

"What do you mean, you told Mason to kill them," Ethan yelled. He raised his gun in a threatening manner as Landon went for his rifle.

It was Micah who intervened this time.

"Killing each other's not going to solve anything." He hobbled over and stood in front of Ethan to shield him.

"Don't think I won't shoot you, old man," Landon said.

"Well, you go right ahead and try," Micah snarled back, holding up his rifle and shaking the barrel at the other man as if bullets weren't threatening enough.

Blu turned away from the feuding men and barked at the open doorway.

Muffled gunshots could be heard in the distance.

"Sounds like they're coming from the cave," Micah said.

"What do you think?" Ethan asked the old-timer.

"Don't know."

Another gunshot echoed out from the throat of the cave.

"That's a Winchester," Ethan said. He glared at Landon. "What's Mason packing?"

"An assault rifle. That's not him."

"Then it has to be Clay. I'm going in there," Ethan said and started for the door.

"I'm coming too." Micah grabbed his crutch.

Blu went for the door.

"No, Blu. You stay here."

The coonhound gave Ethan a puzzled look.

"I don't want you walking into a bullet."

Micah was already out on the porch and was halting around the side of the cabin.

"You better not hurt my dog," Ethan said, but when he looked over at Landon, the man had passed out and was lying flat on the bunk.

Ethan ignored Blu's persistent whining and closed the door after him.

54

When Clay and Mia reached the junction, they couldn't exit the way they had originally come in as there were more little people storming into the cave. They had no choice but to pick another route and ran up the passage that was adjacent to the one they had just come out.

They had no way of knowing where the passage would lead them or if it was going to end up like the other tunnel and become a dead end. If that happened, they would be cornered with no way of escape.

Casey was beginning to cry again which worsened their situation because if they came across another hiding place, the sobbing baby would only give them away.

The footfalls behind them were getting increasingly louder.

They were relieved when they came around a bend and stumbled into an enormous chamber with a high ceiling. To their right was a foul-looking underground body of water and a granite bank full of fifty-gallon casks piled near five wide-belly boilers.

"What is this place?" Mia said, as she stopped running.

"An abandoned distillery," Clay said, frantically looking around. He could see natural sunlight filtering into the cave from somewhere up ahead. "I think that's the way out."

But before they could even go a few feet, a throng of little people poured out of a passageway and cut them off. More tiny feet could be heard, coming out of the tunnel directly behind them.

Clay and Mia watched in horror as the ghoulish creatures began to form a circle around them until they were completely surrounded.

Over a hundred skeletal-looking demons pointed their spears and took a single step toward the center of the circle where Clay and Mia stood helpless.

"What are we going to do?" Mia said, beginning to cry. She zipped her coat up more to cover Casey's head. Somehow, the infant had managed to doze off.

Clay raised his rifle even though there were only a few bullets in the chamber.

"I love you, Mia," he said.

"I love you, too."

The ghouls took another step, shrinking the circle.

55

Mason walked out of the tunnel into a large subterranean cavern, right into the midst of a mob of ghouls that had congregated around Clay and Mia. He could see the couple over the heads of the short creatures.

Clay and Mia saw Mason but didn't immediately acknowledge him, as the menacing bunch of little people hadn't seen him yet. They were too engrossed taunting their captured prey.

And then Ethan ran in, followed by Micah, who was struggling to keep up.

"Oh, my," Micah said, once he saw their predicament. "This ain't good."

The two men were standing about twenty feet away from the outer circle of little people. By now some of the ghouls had turned their heads and were looking at the new arrivals. A few were also staring at Mason, having just realized his presence.

Now that they knew he was there, Mason figured there was no reason not to talk to the others. "Well, I'd say they have us outnumbered twenty to one."

"That's how I see it," Ethan said.

Some of the ghouls glanced back and forth but most of them still had their eyes on the prize in the middle of the ring.

"We have Casey," Mia said. "He's inside my jacket. He's safe, I mean…"

"Thank God for that," Ethan piped in.

"Glad to hear," Mason said.

The monstrous fiends took another step inward, tightening the circumference of the circle; the deadly spears now only five feet away from prodding Clay and Mia.

"Well, I don't see any point in stalling, do you?" Mason called out.

"Nope," Ethan replied.

"Let's do this!" Micah hollered.

Mason charged into the evil throng as Ethan and Micah fired their rifles.

The thunderous gunshots echoed in the granite cathedral akin to a boxing-match bell ringing for the fight to begin.

56

Mason plowed into three ghouls and picked them up in his arms as he ran. As soon as their feet left the ground, the creatures tried to squirm out, twisting in his grip and dropping their lances.

One turned its face completely around and bit into Mason's face. The only thing it got was a mouthful of beard and a head butt from Mason that caved in its forehead.

Charging through the circle, Mason used the ghouls as a shield and ran directly into the demon pigmies on the other side. The spears thrust out in front of the standing ghouls, impaled the three in Mason's clutches. He was fortunate to have escaped being stabbed, released his dead cargo, and yelled to Clay and Mia, "Follow me!"

Clay and Mia dodged the spears and dashed through the hole in their ranks.

But instead of finding an avenue of escape, Clay and Mia quickly realized that they were up against the wall with no way to go as the little people were already breaking away from the circle, and again, were boxing them in.

Not bothering to aim, Mason fired off a couple haphazard shots.

A ghoul hit the dirt when a bullet blasted through its sternum.

Suddenly, Mason was a madman. He grabbed the nearest ghoul, robbed it of its spear, and repeatedly, stabbed the hell out of it.

He yelled a battle cry and rushed the horde.

Clay stood in front of Mia to protect her and their son. He fired off a shot, levered another round, blasted a ghoul at close range and blew off its arm. After going through the motion of ramming another bullet into the chamber and pulling the trigger and nothing happening, Clay used the rifle as a sword and fenced their attackers. He knocked a spear aside and drove the gun muzzle into a ghoul's face.

Micah had run out of ammunition and was stumbling back toward the boilers as a score of ghouls came after him. He staggered up the embankment having to use his crutch as both a means of helping him along and fending the monsters off. He went behind a boiler, and stumbling back, the end of his crutch came up and struck a rusted valve handle and snapped it off at the bib.

He could smell the vapors of high-grade alcohol. A plan came to mind and he reached inside his trouser pocket. He pulled out a flint and struck the metal, creating a spark.

A small explosion erupted.

Micah flew in the air and was thrown ten feet.

The whiskey barrels nearest the ruptured boiler were ablaze and the fire was spreading. Smoke rose off the casks and was drawn upward through the airshafts.

Ethan ran through the surge to see if Micah had survived the blast.

He was grabbed from behind and lifted off his feet. Ethan turned his head and was surprised to see that he was in the death grip of the black bigfoot.

"Not you again," Ethan yelled in the creature's face.

He fought to free himself, but the bigfoot was determined. Before he knew what was happening, they were both in the water. The bigfoot released Ethan and pushed him further into the pool. Ethan splashed down in three feet of dank, polluted water.

The bigfoot lumbered over, grabbed Ethan by the shoulders, and pushed him under.

Ethan tried to pry the creature's hands off, but its grip was too strong. Bubbles started coming out of Ethan's mouth as he struggled to get free.

The liquid contents of the burning barrels gushed out, and like a fiery lava flow, came down in a scorching wave and spilled onto the subterranean pool. A carpet of flames moved rapidly across the body of defiled water.

So intent on killing its foe, the black bigfoot wasn't even aware of the approaching danger until it was suddenly consumed in flames. It yowled with pain and immediately stood up and waded through the watery inferno onto the shore, flailing its burning arms as it ran from the cavern.

Ethan could see the seething blanket of fire on the surface. He rolled over onto his stomach, spun around, and swam as fast as he could underwater until he reached the bank. He vaulted out of the water onto the rocks and rolled a few times to put out the fire clinging to his clothes.

He rushed over to Micah, who was limping over the rocks. Most of the flames had died down as the near-empty casks and boilers were no longer a fuel source.

Micah took one good look at Ethan's smoldering clothes. "Guess that didn't work out so well," he said in a feeble apology.

The little people were already starting to converge.

Ethan looked over and saw Clay and Mia pinned in a corner.

Mason wasn't doing any better. A band of ghouls was moving in for the kill.

"Well, Ethan, it's been a pleasure knowing you," Micah said.

57

Ethan and Micah braced themselves for an attack. Despite everyone's valiant efforts, there were only twenty or so dead ghouls sprawled on the cavern floor, which was hardly a dent in their army.

As the little people formed an encompassing semi-circle entrapment and slowly moved in, Clay and Mia were able to edge along the wall to where Ethan and Micah were making their stand.

Mason growled at the hideous creatures, who returned his taunts with snarls of their own, snapping their teeth and chattering in their nonsensical babble. He kept sidestepping, and eventually joined the rest of the group.

The leader in the snow fox headdress raised its spear—a preparatory signal to charge.

"This is it," Ethan said.

But before the ghoul could instigate the onslaught, there was a loud roar from the mouth of the cave.

Alden rushed in and came to an abrupt halt, slamming his fists on the ground. He glared at the congregation of ghouls and snarled like he was ready to take on the entire legion of little people.

"Well, I'll be," Mason said. "And here I thought he was a coward."

"Go back, Alden!" Micah yelled. "Save yourself."

But instead of heeding his friend's advice, Alden only bellowed louder. To further show his defiance against the ghastly horde, the bigfoot picked up a good-size stone and threw it into the crowd.

The rock was thrown with such force—and precision—that it struck one ghoul in the head then ricocheted into another one's skull.

"Talk about killing two birds with one stone," Micah yelled, pumping his arm in the air.

The ghoulish mob ran at Alden, but it was obvious by his resolve that the bigfoot wasn't going to back down. It was going to be a fight to the death.

And just as Alden was going to be overrun, the bigfoot hunkered down on the ground as a hail of rocks flew over his head and pummeled the first wave of ghouls.

The bone-crushing projectiles punched through their small bodies.

Ethan, Micah, Clay, Mia, and Mason were stunned to see the gray bigfoot clan charge into the cave, pitching heavy rocks with a tremendous degree of accuracy. The little people were falling like saplings in an avalanche.

The bigfoot rushed the shorter creatures, swatting them with their big fists, picking some of them up and hurling their scrawny bodies through the air. Even though they were armed with spears, the ghouls were at a slight height disadvantage as their jabs and thrusts were ineffective on their taller eight-foot-tall opponents. A few bigfoot had suffered minor leg wounds.

It was one thing for a hunting party of little people to overpower a single bigfoot, but it was another thing for them to take on the entire clan.

A bigfoot grabbed the arm of the head ghoul in the white fox headdress just as another bigfoot seized the other arm. The ghoul was yanked apart like a brittle wishbone.

The skirmish was a chaotic cacophony of fierce grunts, clashing bodies, yowls, and roars.

Soon the battlefield was littered with a multitude of little people, so many that the bigfoot were having to step over the heaped bodies in order to combat those that still remained, while the others retreated into the tunnel that led back to the valley.

Ethan took a rough count and estimated that the bigfoot had eliminated two-thirds of the ghouls.

"Good for them," Clay said, remembering the bigfoot skeletal remains that they had found in the little people's boneyard cave. It was long-time the bigfoot got their revenge.

Once the last ghoul had been driven away, the gray bigfoot clan mustered and began ambling toward the cave entrance. As each one passed Alden, they exchanged huffs and grunts—warriors congratulating each other on a battle well fought.

Ethan and Micah started walking toward the mouth of the cave. Clay, Mia, and Mason following right behind.

It wasn't until they were feeling the warmth of the afternoon sun on their faces that a huge shape came out from behind the rocks.

The black bigfoot was grossly disfigured from the fire and its coat was still smoldering. It lurched forward with its arms outstretched to grab Ethan.

A single gunshot sounded and the bigfoot fell to the dirt.

Everyone looked at the man across the clearing.

Landon lowered his rifle and shuffled a couple more steps before he, too, dropped to the ground.

"Landon!" Mason yelled, and ran over to this brother.

Ethan came over and knelt beside the man who had just saved his life. He put his finger on Landon's neck and felt for a pulse. "I'm sorry, Mason."

"I can't believe it. All my brothers are gone."

Mia put a consoling hand on the big man's shoulder. She unzipped her jacket and let Clay take Casey, who was still naked and very grungy.

"We better clean you up, little man. Whew," Clay said, and walked toward the cabin.

Blu came running across the clearing, right up to Ethan.

"Glad to see you, too," Ethan said with a smile as the coonhound licked his face.

58

After Ethan and Mason finished patting the dirt over Landon's grave, Mason used one of the shovels that they had found in the cave and made a cross with a tree branch and the spade's handle. Everyone gathered around the gravesite to show their respect even though no one had any words of condolence to offer.

"Sure you won't come with us?" Ethan asked Micah, while the others got ready for the tedious hike down the mountain.

"I'll be fine," Micah replied. Alden stood next to the old man like a curious child, not really comprehending what was going on but sensing that it was an important moment.

"So you think Alden will stay with you now that he's been accepted by the others?"

"Don't know," Micah said. He looked at the bigfoot and made a couple hand gestures. Alden replied likewise. "He thinks he will."

"That's good. I'd hate to think of you up here all by yourself."

"You're never alone up here."

"No, I guess not. Think you'll have any more trouble from the little people?"

"I imagine so. But it's nothing we can't handle," Micah said, and then put his hand on Alden's shoulder. "Ain't that right, Alden."

The bigfoot managed a grin.

Clay walked over. "We're set to go. Thanks for your help, Micah."

"We mountain folk have to stick together."

Mia joined them. She had fabricated a sling better suited for carrying Casey, who was swaddled to stifle his body odor.

She kissed Micah on the cheek. Then she stepped over, and surprisingly gave Alden a kiss on the cheek as well, despite his repugnant smell.

Micah smiled. "Well, I'll be."

The bigfoot seemed pleased to receive Mia's sign of affection.

Ethan looked over at Mason. "Think you know the way down?"

"I'll get us home," Mason replied confidently.

"Did you hear that sweetie? Soon we'll be home," Mia said to Casey, cradled on her chest. Casey stared up at Mia for a moment then closed his eyes for a nap.

Blu padded over to Alden and licked the bigfoot's hand. Alden reached down and patted the coonhound's head. Once Alden removed his hand, Blu went over and stood beside Ethan.

Everyone bid Micah farewell, for the second time, then, one by one, they filed behind Mason and headed down the trail.

Clay couldn't help noticing the large figures spread out, walking parallel through the trees. Soon everyone was aware.

It was the gray bigfoot clan, giving them safe passage, escorting them down off Stoneclad Mountain.

59

Clay was doing a last touch up on the railing when he heard a car pulling up in front of the house. He put his paintbrush in the can and walked around the side porch.

Ethan gave a friendly wave as an old model station wagon drove over and parked next to his Scout truck. Blu was eagerly waiting, wagging his tail so fast, it was a miracle it didn't fly off.

A woman in her early forties got out of the car. She had raven black hair tied back in a long ponytail and was wearing a flannel shirt and jeans.

"Ethan, what a pleasant surprise."

"How's that sister of yours?" Ethan inquired.

"Hates Porterville like a passion, but she's been saying that for years."

She went to the back of the station wagon, opened the rear cargo door, and let out two bluetick coonhounds that jumped down on the ground. Blu immediately ran over and the dogs started their sniffing routine before they started jumping around to play.

Clay walked down the porch steps and approached the vehicles.

"Alberta, I want you to meet my nephew, Clay," Ethan said.

"Proud to meet you," Alberta said and put out her hand.

Clay started to extend his hand then noticed it was covered with paint.

"Don't mind that," Alberta said and shook Clay's hand. "So, I take it, you two aren't working on the roof?"

Clay didn't know what to say and looked at Ethan.

"Actually, we finished replacing those shingles. Thought we would spruce the place up before you got back."

"Well, thank you, Ethan."

The three coonhounds were racing about in the nearby field.

"Are those Blu's parents?" Clay asked.

"That they are," Alberta replied. "Samson and Beulah."

"Blu's a fine dog," Clay said.

"How's Blu been?" Alberta asked. "Anymore seizures?"

"He had one episode," Ethan said. "But he got over it pretty quick."

"So, anything exciting happen while I was away?" Alberta asked as they walked up the porch steps to the front door.

"You might say that," Clay said.

They went inside and walked through the living room into the small kitchen.

Alberta glanced around at the new cabinets and the minor alterations.

"Ethan, you outdid yourself."

"I was hoping you'd like it."

"How about I make us some coffee," Alberta said, filling a coffee pot with water at the sink.

"All right," Ethan said, pulling up a chair. Clay sat down at the table across from his uncle.

Alberta put the pot on the stove and turned on the burner. She sat down next to Ethan and smiled. "So you two want to catch me up?"

60

Since their return, Mia had bathed Casey three separate times with bar soap in the outdoor shower and scrubbed him until his skin was pink, but after she dried him off, he still smelled. She tried sprinkling him all over with talcum powder, even some perfume from an old bottle that Clay had given her when they were first dating. Nothing seemed to work.

It was if the skunk-like odor was coming out of his tiny pores; a foulness bleeding through a colander.

Mia prayed it would wear off in time as it was becoming unbearable for her to be around her own son.

Mia decided to pull the playpen out on the porch and placed Casey inside. As it was a warm afternoon, Mia thought it would speed up the process of ridding her son of the god-awful smell if she didn't dress Casey in anything but a diaper.

She kept the front door open to further air out the cabin, and so she could keep an eye on her son while she did her baking.

Mia added some flour into a mixing bowl, a couple eggs, seasoning, and some canned milk. She took a whisk, and after a minute or two, beat the ingredients into a thick batter.

Mia glanced over at the open door.

Casey wasn't inside his playpen.

She dropped the bowl on the kitchen table and rushed across the room onto the porch.

The pillow—she always used to block off the space with the missing slats—had been pushed out and was lying on the porch deck.

Mia went to the railing and frantically looked around, thinking her infant son couldn't have gotten far. She raced down the steps.

"Casey!" she yelled, dashing over to the outdoor shower, and then glancing over at the car. He was nowhere to be seen.

Mia tried not to panic but she couldn't help herself as she sprinted down the side of the cabin. What if it was happening all over again?

She was nearing the rear of the cabin when she saw Casey waddling across the short grass.

Her heart sunk when a giant shadow loomed over her son.

"Casey!" Mia screamed.

Powerful arms scooped up the toddler.

The bigfoot ambled over to Mia and handed over her boy.

"Thank you, Alden," Mia said. She turned and saw Micah with his crutch, limping out of the forest.

"He insisted we visit," Micah said. "Damn if that ain't a long trip."

"Oh my God, you must be completely worn out."

"That I am," Micah replied.

"Come inside and I'll fix you something."

"We could use some grub."

"Clay and Ethan should be back soon."

As Micah and Alden headed around the side of the cabin, Mia glanced back at the edge of the forest. A breeze had picked up, shaking the bushes and rattling the leaves on the trees. It was as if the mountain had suddenly come alive.

She held on tight to her son and watched nervously, afraid of what might be coming out of those woods next.

THE END

ABOUT THE AUTHOR

Gerry Griffiths lives in San Jose, California with his family and their five rescue dogs and a cat. He is a Horror Writers Association member and has over thirty published short stories in various anthologies and magazines, as well as a short story collection entitled *Creatures*. He is also the author of two novels, *Silurid* and *Death Crawlers*, both published by Severed Press.

CHECK OUT OTHER GREAT HORROR NOVELS

BLACK FRIDAY
by Michael Hodges

Jared the kleptomaniac, Chike the unemployed IT guy, Patricia the shopaholic, and Jeff the meth dealer are trapped inside a Chicago supermall on Black Friday. Bridgefield Mall empties during a fire alarm, and most of the shoppers drive off into a strange mist surrounding the mall parking lot. They never return. Chike and his group try calling friends and family, but their smart phones won't work, not even Twitter. As the mist creeps closer, the mall lights flicker and surge. Bulbs shatter and spray glass into the air. Unsettling noises are heard from within the mist, as the meth dealer becomes unhinged and hunts the group within the mall. Cornered by the mist, and hunted from within, Chike and the survivors must fight for their lives while solving the mystery of what happened to Bridgefield Mall. Sometimes, a good sale just isn't worth it.

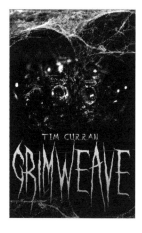

GRIMWEAVE
by Tim Curran

In the deepest, darkest jungles of Indochina, an ancient evil is waiting in a forgotten, primeval valley. It is patient, monstrous, and bloodthirsty. Perfectly adapted to its hot, steaming environment, it strikes silent and stealthy, it chosen prey: human. Now Michael Spiers, a Marine sniper, the only survivor of a previous encounter with the beast, is going after it again. Against his better judgement, he is made part of a Marine Force Recon team that will hunt it down and destroy it.

The hunters are about to become the hunted.

CHECK OUT OTHER GREAT HORROR NOVELS

DEATH CRAWLERS
by Gerry Griffiths

Worldwide, there are thought to be 8,000 species of centipede, of which, only 3,000 have been scientifically recorded. The venom of Scolopendra gigantea—the largest of the arthropod genus found in the Amazon rainforest—is so potent that it is fatal to small animals and toxic to humans. But when a cargo plane departs the Amazon region and crashes inside a national park in the United States, much larger and deadlier creatures escape the wreckage to roam wild, reproducing at an astounding rate. Entomologist, Frank Travis solicits small town sheriff Wanda Rafferty's help and together they investigate the crash site. But as a rash of gruesome deaths befalls the townsfolk of Prospect, Frank and Wanda will soon discover how vicious and cunning these new breed of predators can be. Meanwhile, Jake and Nora Carver, and another backpacking couple, are venturing up into the mountainous terrain of the park. If only they knew their fun-filled weekend is about to become a living nightmare.

THE PULLER
by Michael Hodges

Matt Kearns has two choices: fight or hide. The creature in the orchard took the rest. Three days ago, he arrived at his favorite place in the world, a remote shack in Michigan's Upper Peninsula. The plan was to mourn his father's death and figure out his life. Now he's fighting for it. An invisible creature has him trapped. Every time Matt tries to flee, he's dragged backwards by an unseen force. Alone and with no hope of rescue, Matt must escape the Puller's reach. But how do you free yourself from something you cannot see?

CHECK OUT OTHER GREAT
HORROR NOVELS

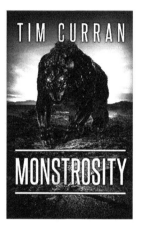

MONSTROSITY
by Tim Curran

The Food. It seeped from the ground, a living, gushing, teratogenic nightmare. It contaminated anything that ate it, causing nature to run wild with horrible mutations, creating massive monstrosities that roam the land destroying towns and cities, feeding on livestock and human beings and one another. Now Frank Bowman, an ordinary farmer with no military skills, must get his children to safety. And that will mean a trip through the contaminated zone of monsters, madmen, and The Food itself. Only a fool would attempt it. Or a man with a mission.

THE SQUIRMING
by Jack Hamlyn

You are their hosts

You are their food.

The parasites came out of nowhere, squirming horrors that enslaved the human race.They turned the population into mindless pack animals, psychotic cannibalistic hordes whose only purpose was to feed them.

Now with the human race teetering at the edge of extinction, extermination teams are fighting back, killing off the parasites and their voracious hosts. Taking them out one by one in violent, bloody encounters.

The future of mankind is at stake.

And time is running out.

Printed in Great Britain
by Amazon

62259389R00109